"Have you no shame at all?"

"My conscience is quite clear, thank you, Alex," Hope replied crisply.

"Do you like playing games with people?" His icy glare impaled her.

"A girl's got to amuse herself."

"Is that what you were doing with me?"

The flicker in Alex's hooded eyes made Hope feel uneasy, but she wasn't going to backpedal now. "Well, I've got to do *something* for the next month, and I do find *older* men so attractive," she confided with her best come-hither smile.

Alex reached out to her, and glimpsed shock in her wide blue eyes before he kissed her....

Wanted: three husbands for three sisters!

Anna, Lindy and Hope—triplet sisters and the best, the closest, of friends. Physically, these three women may look alike, but their personalities are very different! Anna is lively and vivacious, Lindy is the practical one and Hope sparkles with style and sophistication.

But they have one thing in common: each sister is about to meet a man she will tantalize, torment and finally tame! And when these spirited women find true love, they'll become the most beautiful triplet brides....

Turn the page to enjoy the third Lacey sister's story as Hope meets her match!

Kim Lawrence

AN INNOCENT AFFAIR

HARLEQUIN®

TORONTO • NEW YORK • LONDON
AMSTERDAM • PARIS • SYDNEY • HAMBURG
STOCKHOLM • ATHENS • TOKYO • MILAN • MADRID
PRAGUE • WARSAW • BUDAPEST • AUCKLAND

ISBN 0-373-12114-8

AN INNOCENT AFFAIR

First North American Publication 2000.

Copyright © 1998 by Kim Lawrence.

Visit us at www.eHarlequin.com

Printed in U.S.A.

CHAPTER ONE

'AUNT Beth didn't cry at all.' There was implied criticism in the soft voice. 'I *always* cry at weddings.'

Hope didn't think the lace-edged handkerchief her fellow guest shook gently would have been much serious use. On closer scrutiny she couldn't detect any tell-tale smears in the smooth, matt make-up.

'Including your own, I expect.' She regretted the dry comment the moment she made it; the shaky condition of her cousin's marriage was well known. The trouble was she didn't like Tricia and never had; she was shallow, pretentious and totally lacking in spontaneity. Being in her company solidly for the past half-hour had worn her tolerance level down.

'Roger is in Geneva; he has business there.' The brittle defences were clearly on show. 'I miss him, but I don't expect *you* to understand about the special closeness marriage brings.'

Hope let the insult wash over her; she'd weathered worse over the past weeks. Besides, this time she'd deserved a reprimand. You're a cow, Hope Lacey, Hope told herself with disgust. Roger's 'business' was a ten-years-younger version of his wife, and everyone knew it. Two bright patches of colour had emerged on her cousin's cheeks.

'Then we'll have to take lots of pictures to show Roger how gorgeous you look, won't we?' she said, her generous personality reasserting itself. 'Smile,' she instructed brightly. 'Anna has instructed me to point this thing at everything that moves. She insists that the of-

5

ficial photos never give an accurate impression of any occasion. Too cosmetic.'

'Anna always has been a bit odd.'

Hope bit back the instinctive scathing retort that hovered on her tongue. 'Well, she certainly has appalling timing. Fancy giving birth to twins twelve hours before your sister gets married.'

Hope knew that Anna's absence had been the one cloud on Lindy's horizon today. The triplets had a close relationship, and on today of all days Rosalind had wanted them all to be together.

'Twins!' Tricia shuddered, and from her expression Hope instinctively knew she was about to receive a detailed history of her cousin's own labour.

'Well, it's less dramatic than triplets.' Hope heroically fixed an interested expression on her face as Tricia launched into a detailed account. She found it hard to keep the glazed look from her eyes.

The story she was hearing didn't do much for her own maternal instincts, such as they were! It could be I'm meant to be a maiden aunt, she reflected. Her smile faltered. Tricia hadn't even got to the part where her waters broke yet. This might be a long haul! Look on it as penance for that catty remark, Hope, she told herself severely. Poor Tricia. Considering how many women she knew who, like Tricia, were hanging on for grim death to the shreds of miserable marriages, she wondered that the institution was so popular.

Twenty minutes later Hope had her long silk skirts in one hand and a fortifying glass of champagne in the other. She was heading towards the small marquee set on her parents' lawn from where the foot-tapping music emanated.

Her attention was diverted before she'd reached her destination. He wasn't the tallest figure standing in the small group, but he was easily the most arresting. As he began to speak, using his hands to emphasise a point— no wide, sweeping gestures for this man; his hands inscribed economic, precise gestures in the air—Hope pulled the camera from around her neck and began clicking.

When he turned his head and looked directly at her, for once Hope's poise deserted her. She turned quickly away, guilty as a child caught spying on her elders.

Great move, she silently cursed, trying to ram the lens cap back onto the camera. 'Damn thing!' She bent down on the damp ground, trying to recapture the item.

'Can I help?'

They both reached for the lens cover at the same instant, and her fingers touched the tips of a much stronger pair of hands. Hands that matched the powerful image of the man, with neatly manicured square fingernails. The hands of an artisan and not a philosopher. It was the impression of immense strength Alex Matheson emanated that had first caught her attention. She fleetingly imagined the intense vitality he exuded had transferred itself along the nerve-endings in her fingertips.

'Thank you.' She turned her hand palm-up to receive the cap. 'It doesn't belong to me,' she explained with a warm smile.

There was none of the immediate recognition on his face that Hope was accustomed to. She was one of an elite band of international supermodels, and her face made her public property. Strangers always made a big thing of identifying her, and after the unpleasant media coverage she'd received just lately there couldn't be many people in the country who didn't know who she was. At least he wasn't condemning her out of hand, the way a lot of strangers did, which disposed Hope to think well of him.

'It's a good camera.' His deep voice had a gravelly, husky quality which was incredibly attractive. They straightened up in unison.

'And idiot-proof, or so Adam says. Adam's my brother-in-law, or one of them. I've got two now.' This notion was still novel enough to make her grin.

'I know Adam.'

'Of course you do.' It was a small community, and as the main employer in the area Alex was bound to know most people. Adam and he no doubt moved in the same social circles. 'Anna had the twins in the early hours of the morning. Boys. She didn't want announcements or anything today. She insists this is Lindy's day. Lindy and Sam stopped by at the hospital on their way from the church; that's why they were late.'

Alex nodded. 'I had heard about the babies. You're cold,' he said as she shivered. 'Shall we go inside?' He turned towards the farmhouse rather than the marquee, but Hope didn't demur; there was no competition when it came to the comparative attractions of the music and Alex Matheson! He was fascinating with a capital F.

'I'm wearing my thermal underwear under this, but if anyone asks you to be a bridesmaid in winter have your excuses ready.'

'I think that scenario is unlikely, but thanks for the advice. Tell me, are you really?'

The warmth enfolded her like a warm blanket as they walked into the farmhouse. Or was it the warmth and interest in his grey eyes? He had a peculiarly direct way of looking at a person, which could be vaguely unsettling, but Hope rather liked it. The less energetically inclined were clustered in groups in the unpretentious ground-floor rooms of her parents' eighteenth-century farmhouse. The wedding was an intentionally small, intimate occasion with an emphasis on informality.

'Am I really what?'

Alex's eyes briefly touched the long line of her thighs outlined by the rose-coloured clinging fabric. He tried to picture long johns underneath the fine layer and found his mental picture kept shifting to frivolous lace and shimmering satin.

'Wearing thermal underwear?' He delivered the line straight-faced, but she liked the lick of humour in his eyes. It was refreshing to meet a man who wasn't over-awed by her reputation, or at least one who was interested. He was interested, wasn't he? A bizarre thought suddenly occurred to her...

'Do you know who I am? Oh, God, that sounds awful.' She winced. 'I mean, people—men—tend to treat me...' She struggled in vain to explain what she meant. How did a girl say that a lot of the nice men were too scared to approach her, and that the sort of men who wanted her as a trophy left her cold, without sounding wildly conceited?

'Like a goddess?' he interjected smoothly. The humour was more pronounced now. 'Understandable.'

His grey eyes made a slow but comprehensive journey from her toes to the tip of her gleaming head. He looked as if he approved of what he saw. That in itself wasn't unusual—most men did like looking at Hope—it was the fact she *wanted* him to like what he saw that made the experience strange.

'But not very desirable.' He *was* interested. A hiccough of excitement made her heartbeat kick up another gear. She was well accustomed to meeting interesting and important people, but there was something about this man that put him in a league of his own.

'I'm not being reprimanded for not showing due reverence, then?'

Hope chuckled, a warm rich sound. She stopped

abruptly, a frown wrinkling her brow. 'I don't quite re-member—you're not married, are you?' Size sevens straight in the mouth, Hope—nice touch!

Alex didn't seem to find her direct approach undesir-able. 'Not even slightly.' There was the faintest of quiv-ers around his firm rather delicious mouth.

'Good. Can we be friends?'

Hope Lacey, he decided, blinking, had a smile that could stop a charging rhino in its tracks. She really is enchanting, and I'm a push-over, he concluded wryly.

'Friends' had a nice, uncomplicated sound, but the feelings this man was arousing within her were far from simple. 'The last time I met you I probably called you Mr Matheson.'

Alex winced; he'd been trying to forget that. 'You did.' He doubted they'd ever exchanged more than a passing greeting. There had been very little common ground between a man in his late twenties and a teen-ager. If he recalled Hope at all it was as one of the coltish daughters of his neighbours, Beth and Charlie Lacey.

'I was in my teens then, and you were?' He had the sort of face that was impossible to give an age too. His body certainly showed no signs of wear and tear!

'I'm forty now—next week, actually.'

He was a man who got directly to the point, Hope noted appreciatively. There was quite a lot to appreciate about him. He wasn't pretty, more arresting, she con-cluded. His features were strong and angular, his high cheekbones had a Slavic cast and his jaw was square and firm. His Roman nose had obviously been broken at some point, but Hope found she didn't disapprove of this irregularity.

'I'm twenty-seven. It's amazing how time has dimin-ished the age-gap.'

'Has it?' His lips compressed in a cynical smile and Hope noticed with interest that though his upper lip was firm, his bottom lip was altogether more sensually full.

'Certainly,' she replied confidently. 'Unless you still want me to call you Mr Matheson?'

'Call me Alex. But it won't do anything to lessen the age-gap. And shall I call you Lacey?'

'That's a professional thing; my friends call me Hope.' Someone murmured an apology and Alex moved aside to let them pass. He had the sort of shoulders that could single-handedly block most hallways; they were massive, as was his chest, and it made him seem taller than he actually was.

She stood five-eleven in her bare feet, and nose to nose, as they were now, she could look him directly in the eye. Alex put one hand out to brace himself against the wall as the guests moved past. This close, his physical presence was literally overwhelming.

'I bet you can't buy a suit off the peg.' She closed her eyes and allowed herself a small groan. 'I'm not always so personal.' She'd spoken in response to a surge of unexpected panic that had attacked her.

'You can be as personal as you like with me, Hope. I like directness. You're right. I have my clothes made to measure.'

He had to shave twice a day too, she realised, noticing the shadow across his jaw. She was gripped by a sudden and frighteningly strong urge to sink her fingers into his lush dark hair.

'This is silly,' she breathed with a frown.

'And dangerous,' he agreed drily.

Hope stared in a dazed fashion into his eyes. As she watched, the pupil expanded until it almost met the dark rim that surrounded his grey iris. Her eyes slid slowly to his mouth…she licked her dry lips nervously. It ought to be illegal for one man to have this much earthy sex appeal.

'You too?' She was amazed he'd replied to her soft self-recrimination.

The lines bracketing his strong mouth deepened as he smiled a little grimly in response. His expression remained enigmatic. She instinctively recognised that he wasn't the sort of person who permitted his emotions to rise close to the surface.

'Your halo's crooked.' He inclined his head towards her corn-coloured hair.

The puzzlement vanished from her face as her fingers touched the coronet of dried rosebuds that was wound into the Pre-Raphaelite curls her hair had been teased into. The tiny village church had been lovingly decorated with garlands of the same pink roses, bound together with lichen and rosemary on a base of rich, rosy velvet.

'It was a lovely service,' she remarked dreamily. 'Lindy looked beautiful.'

'I suppose she did.'

'Suppose!' she echoed indignantly.

'I was looking at you. You looked like a glowing Botticelli angel.'

This was unexpected enough to take her breath away. He wasn't the sort of man she would have associated with flowery compliments. 'I'm no angel.'

'No,' he agreed in that slow, deliberate manner of his. 'That would be boring. I can't abide being bored, even by an angel.'

'Looks don't compensate for lack of character, then?'

'You've got both.' He spoke calmly, as if he were simply stating the obvious.

'Some people take convincing.'

'I'm a quick learner.'

'Talking to you makes a person dizzy,' she gasped. 'Are *you* always so personal?'

'I'll do the weather and the economy if you prefer.'

'How about what a lovely wedding it was?'

'I don't like weddings, but, as such occasions go, this wasn't too bad. Tell me, how did you manage to keep the affair secret? I thought when the likes of Sam Rourke married, the press from every continent would be camped on the doorstep.'

'Sam's very good at laying false trails,' she said, smiling affectionately when she thought of her new brother-in-law. Sam was an actor of international repute, and millions of women would shed a tear, or several, when they learned he'd married. 'Also, the invitations weren't sent out until Wednesday, and they listed the groom as "Patrick S. Rourke," which happens to be his other name. I'm surprised a busy man like you could drop everything and come at such short notice.'

'I had nothing else planned. I got back from Saudi yesterday. It was good of your parents to invite me.' He didn't add he'd had every intention of putting in the briefest of appearances.

'You weathered the recession, then?' Alex Matheson's firm built distinctive handmade cars. The unapologetically nostalgic lines of the sports cars were instantly recognisable and they were much sought after.

'Happily, yes.' He could afford to be confident; there was a five-year waiting list for each of the three models they produced. 'And how long are you home for, Hope?'

It could be the quiet, firm responses of the couple in the church had softened his brain. Better for them both if she was off to some exotic fashion shoot before they responded to this attraction. Whichever way you looked at it, Hope Lacey was too young for him, Alex reflected. He'd half expected to be disillusioned when he spoke to her. If he was honest, he'd wanted to be. A healthy dose of reality had seemed the perfect cure for the fascination that had hit him the instant she'd walked into the church. Far from curing him, he found the reality attractive; she was surprisingly natural and mature. Warm, funny— He pulled himself up short. The list could get tiresomely long.

'I'm at home for the next month.'

Fate wasn't going to do him any favours! Alex noted the small, smug smile that curved her beautiful lips. Well, she had every right to be confident about her ability to bewitch a man, he silently conceded.

'Resting?' One winged dark brow rose teasingly.

'Well, it's always a temptation to do everything you're offered, but you reach the point when you realise there isn't much point burning out just to bank every available dollar. I'm a bit more discriminating these days.'

'You can afford to be.'

Hope didn't dispute this. Modelling had made her financially secure. 'I've been lucky and I work hard. This film might be a new start for me.' It was a month since she'd finished the round of TV and radio chat shows to promote the film. She was excited and apprehensive about the American premiere soon.

'You play opposite Sam Rourke?'

Hope nodded. 'I introduced Lindy to him, so if anything goes wrong in Eden they'll blame me, no doubt. Come on, let's get some champagne before it's all gone.' She touched his arm lightly and he followed her into the kitchen.

'Hope, dear, there you are.' Beth Lacey, her hands deep in a sink of soapy water, smiled at her daughter. 'Hello, Alex. I hope you're having a good time?'

'I'm being well looked after.'

'Do you mind washing a few glasses for me, Hope? We had a major breakage. I should really remind Lindy she ought to be getting changed.'

'Sure, off you go, Mum.'

Hope tied an incongruous striped apron over her bridesmaid dress. 'The spare bubbly's in the dairy,' she told Alex. 'Third door along,' she added, inclining her head towards the passageway behind him. She immersed her hands in the water and gave a sigh. 'Why is it your nose always itches when you haven't got a spare hand?' she complained.

'Let me,' he offered. Before Hope realised what he was about to do Alex leant over and rubbed the tip of her straight nose, which fell somewhere in between the cute and aquiline categories. 'Better?'

Hope gave a hoarse grunt of assent. I'm staring so hard I'm probably cross-eyed, she decided ruefully. He smells awfully good...she appreciatively breathed in the spicy, faintly lemony scent of his cologne mingled with the musky, masculine odour of his warm body. If she could distil what this man did to her quivering stomach muscles, she'd be a very rich alchemist. Yes, alchemy had the right ring to it. There was certainly something mystically marvellous about the way she was feeling. Come clean, Hope, she reprimanded herself. Earthy and raw was much closer to the truth!

His hand dropped away, but not completely. His thumb ran slowly across the cushiony softness of her slightly parted lips. 'You're no plastic clone.'

This peculiar comment enabled Hope to pull free from the strangely hypnotic haze that made her loath to withdraw from the light contact.

'Is that your idea of a compliment?' His hand still hadn't fallen away completely; now the palm of his hand rested ever so lightly against the curve of her jaw. 'Because if so…'

'You know what I mean—the sort of blond bimbo-types that they churn out, all teeth and silicone.'

Hope gave a shout of laughter. 'That's a bad case of stereotypes you've got there. There's room at the top for variety and individuality. In fact, I think both are essential.' She flicked soapsuds at him.

Her action seemed to startle him. Perhaps Alex Matheson wasn't the sort of man people laughed at or teased? He met the humour shining in her blue eyes and his immense shoulders visibly relaxed.

He shrugged. 'I don't know much about acting or modelling.'

'You just know what you like?' she suggested, tongue firmly in her cheek.

'And what I don't like. To tell you the honest truth, the idea of silicone…bits gives me the creeps,' he confessed. This sent Hope into a fresh spate of giggles.

'You're so…so quaint,' she gasped, wiping tears of mirth from her eyes.

Alex paused in the act of mopping the soapy suds from his sleek hair and gaped at her. 'Quaint?' he repeated in a strange tone.

'In the nicest possible way,' she assured him kindly.

'I'm relieved.'

'Actually, for models, too much up top can be a nuisance,' she confided. 'Clothes hang better on an androgynous frame.'

'You're not androgynous.' His eyes dwelt fleetingly on the ample proof of this statement.

'I'm not the waif type,' she agreed. 'I'm meant to be the athletic, wholesome, sexy type,' she explained, very matter-of-factly.

'And are you?'

'I play a mean game of tennis,' she replied selectively.

Her caution brought a grin to his face, making him appear younger and less severe. He really ought to grin more often, she decided appreciatively. 'Perhaps we could play some time?'

Hope could field sexual innuendo with the best of them, but to her amazement she felt the colour creep inexorably up her neck until her face was aflame.

'I expect you like to win?'

Alex withdrew his fascinated gaze from her crimson cheeks with difficulty. 'Doesn't everyone?' Her veneer of sophistication was much thinner than he'd imagined.

'I don't possess the killer instinct.'

'You think I do?'

Hope placed the last glass on the draining board and shook the moisture off her hands. 'If I say yes, you'll accuse me of stereotyping you as the hard-nosed businessman—ruthless and incapable of compassion.' As she spoke it struck her forcibly how very easily he *could* be slotted into that category. It wasn't just that he was physically formidable; the stamp of authority went gene-deep in him. He was a man accustomed to making what he wanted to happen occur.

He saw the flicker of uncertainty cross her face. 'I draw the line at homicide.'

'That's a comfort.'

'It would seem I'm woefully uneducated about your life.'

'Don't worry, I don't know much about building cars.'

'We could exchange information and improve our general knowledge,' he suggested silkily.

'Are we talking a date?' A cautious smile trembled on her lips. It was scary how much his reply meant to her.

'Tryst, assignation, rendezvous...' She was mature for

her age, and there was nothing artificial about this girl—
woman, he firmly corrected himself. The need to justify
his response was strong.

'I'd like that.' She sounded cool and collected, having
firmly quashed the inclination to jump on the table and
dance.

'Good.' The gleam of ruthlessness in his grey eyes,
the one that bothered her, was back. 'Where did you say
the champagne was?'

'How did it go, Hope?' Charlie managed to get a quiet
moment alone with his daughter once the guests had
begun to disperse.

'Better than I expected.'

'You'll be yesterday's news before long,' he com-
forted her.

Hope nodded. She'd managed to be philosophical
about the gossip that followed in her wake at the moment.

The whole world thought she was having an affair
with Lloyd Elliot, the producer of the film she'd just
starred in. She'd read countless articles about how she'd
heartlessly broken up his marriage. Her motivation, so
said the general consensus, had been to further her career. Lloyd's estranged wife, the tempestuous singer
Dallas, had given some very moving 'brave victim'
interviews. If Hope hadn't known she and Lloyd had
been living separate lives for years, she'd have been
touched herself!

When Hope had agreed to divert public attention from
the *real* new love of Lloyd's life, she hadn't realised just
how much that decision was going to affect her and her
family. It was too late to wonder, with hindsight,
whether her decision might have been different if she
had known. But her family knew the truth, and before

long, when Lloyd went public about the real object of his affections, so would everyone else.

'It'll be a relief,' she admitted to her father. 'You certainly get to know who your real friends are. And today wasn't as bad as I thought it was going to be, unless I'm getting over the paranoia.'

'It seemed you were making a new friend.'

'Someone doesn't miss much,' Hope responded drily; the casual tone didn't fool her for a second.

'Your mother did happen to mention that you had Alex Matheson in tow.'

'I wouldn't phrase it quite like that. He's an interesting man.'

'Not an easy man to get to know, though—aloof... He's never really gotten involved in village life. I've known him since he was a boy, and he always supports local charities and fund-raisers very generously, but...' He frowned, trying to put into words his doubts about Alex Matheson. Women were strange creatures, they probably found the fact the man was something of an enigma attractive.

Hope was torn between irritation and exasperated affection. Sometimes her parents forgot how long she'd been out in the big bad world.

'So, he's a private person. At least he didn't treat me like some sort of scarlet woman! There's no need to look so worried, Dad. I'm not about to do anything stupid.' Am I? she silently asked herself. Wasn't there something very appealing about doing something *very* stupid with Alex Matheson?

Charlie Lacey enfolded his daughter in a bear-like hug. 'I know you're a sensible girl,' he said gruffly.

Am I? Hope wondered, recalling with a shiver the smouldering expression in Alex's eyes as he'd left.

CHAPTER TWO

THE curls that had escaped the fat plait Hope had tied her hair in were tugged this way and that in the gusting winds. Her light waterproof jacket cut out the worst of it, but her nose felt distinctly pink as she strode sure-footedly over the hillside.

Bishop's Crag was a well-known landmark; it was the highest point for several miles around. She knew the spot well, but it had been years since she'd been here. She paused to get her breath and inhaled deeply. She'd forgotten how beautiful her home county was. She was surprised to see a light dusting of early snow on this high ground.

Alex Matheson was different; she had to give him that! No romantic candlelight to sweep a girl off her feet for him. Possibly this was some sort of endurance test he put all his prospective girlfriends through. The thought made her grin. Then a shaft of shock swept through her as she recognised the direction her thoughts had been taking her.

She didn't have boyfriends. At least she hadn't in a long time. There had been the brief, intense involvement with Hugh Gilmour, her first agent, but that had been short-lived. Since then she hadn't felt the need, or desire, to become involved with any man. She'd made a few good friends within the industry, and some of them were men, but she'd never felt inclined to push friendship farther.

'Boyfriend.' The wind tugged the word from her lips.

No, she shook her head, there was nothing vaguely boyish about Alex; he was all man.

She was about to continue when a flicker of movement on the periphery of her vision caught her attention. To her left, on higher ground, just below a clump of trees, their skeletal winter frames permanently bent by the constant buffeting of high winds, he stood—a solitary figure who would never be bent by any storm.

She automatically followed the skyward direction of his stare. A dark dot appeared to fall quite literally from the sky before wheeling at an impossible angle and skimming the ground. It landed on Alex's outstretched arm.

Awed by this primal display of aerobatics, Hope waved to the solitary figure. He didn't respond, but she put this down to the fact he was handling the bird on his wrist.

'Why didn't you tell me you had a hawk?' she panted as she finally reached his side. Hope's cheeks were glowing from her exertion. Her fascinated eyes touched the bird on his gauntleted hand before she smiled at the man.

'She's a falcon.' There had been more warmth in the beady, unblinking stare of the bird of prey.

She didn't need to be psychic to experience a premonition of dread. The wind ruffled and tugged at his thick hair, but his face was as hard as the rock he was balanced upon. He looked as much at home in the bleak landscape as his bird. He extended his arm and the creature took flight.

'Aren't you afraid she won't come back?'

'She occasionally absconds, but she always comes back to me.' With a minute alteration of his features he managed to imply that the concept of such faithfulness was beyond Hope's grasp.

'Are you going to tell me what's wrong?' All those romantic scenarios she'd built up in her head were disintegrating under the ruthless glare of reality. It was ironic that she'd smiled stoically through the mud-slinging of the past few weeks and now all this man had to do was flare a nostril and she felt her blood pressure rising and her heart bleeding!

'Why should anything be wrong, Hope?'

His sarcastic drawl made her feel helpless and angry. The last dregs of her bubbling anticipation drained away under the cold glare of his eyes.

'That's what I'd like to know. And will you get down off that damned crag? It's impossible to talk to someone who's looming over me,' she responded, exasperated and dismayed by his peculiar attitude. Could this be the same man she had spoken to yesterday? 'If you're having second thoughts, fine—but is there any need to freeze me out?'

Looking at her glowing, apparently innocent face brought a sneer to his lips. He jumped down from the rocky crag with one lithe movement.

This display of agility in such a big man took Hope by surprise. If she'd imagined he would be less intimidating at eye level she soon discovered her mistake—controlled fury was the only way to describe the expression on his face. Her bewilderment and confusion were snowballing.

Over his shoulder she saw the falcon drop onto a small bird, probably a pigeon. Her imagination conjured up cruel talons tearing into the fragile frame of its prey. She shuddered. They made a good pair, man and bird. If he'd had talons she could readily imagine him sinking them into her.

'Why did you ask me if I was married?'

'Because I don't...' Her voice suddenly trailed off.

Things slipped unpleasantly into place. 'You hadn't read any of the articles about—'

'About you and your married lover. A fact you took full advantage of,' he observed derisively. 'I did tell you I'd been out of the country.'

'That's me—never let an opportunity to snare a poor, defenceless male pass me by. Of course, it would have been more satisfying if you'd had a wife and ten children.' She spat the words from between clenched teeth.

To think I was impressed he hadn't been influenced by the scurrilous tales! To think I thought he was warm and interesting! The fact that he was still the most virile male she'd ever met only intensified her disappointment. 'An invalid mother would have been icing on the cake.' Flippancy covered the pain of having her eyes opened to his true personality.

'I can't abide fakes,' he responded in an austere manner that made her temper climb to new heights.

'I can't abide sanctimonious bores!'

'Your family must have been going through hell.'

'Thanks to nasty-minded creeps like you, they probably still are!'

'Don't try to transfer the guilt you feel to me, Hope. I suppose it's something that you're still *capable* of feeling guilt...'

'And still capable of wrapping a sucker like you around my little finger.' She'd hit the nail right on the head there; she could see it from the flash of rage in his eyes. That was all his outrage was about: he didn't like the idea his judgement could be flawed. The great Alex Matheson didn't get taken for a ride by anyone!

'I'm sure you've had a great deal of practice; you're very professional.'

She gasped, as if the slow, deliberate drawl had been a blow. The sound of her open palm as it struck the side of his face was like a whip-crack. 'Oh, God, look what you made me do!' She barely had time to shriek the words before the bird streaked past her face. Alex knocked her to the ground and the creature sped away.

He squatted beside her as she raised her head and groaned. 'It's only a superficial scratch. You were lucky.'

Her fingers curled in the mossy soil. 'Break out the champagne to celebrate,' she croaked. She gave a whimper and her head dropped once more. A sheen of cold perspiration covered her pale skin and beaded along her upper lip. She battled to overcome the waves of nausea.

'There won't be a scar.' She flinched back as he touched the side of her cheek. 'It barely broke the skin.'

'It's not that.' She took several deep breaths and prayed she wouldn't disgrace herself totally. 'I'm going to throw up and it's all your fault.' This was always the aftermath of a brief flash of blind rage, this humiliating physical helplessness.

At least he had the sense to give her some privacy. As creeps went, he was fairly sensitive. A few minutes later she got to her feet and climbed the rocky outcrop he was sitting upon.

'Are you pregnant?' That made her lose her footing. Arms windmilling wildly, she managed not to fall, though that could hardly be more humiliating than losing her breakfast in front of him.

'I'd hardly be blaming you if I was, would I?' she responded, choosing a flattish piece of ground to sit upon, not too close to him. She felt the slight welt where the bird's claws had grazed her face. She took out a tissue and spat on it. 'Didn't I read somewhere that saliva's antiseptic?' she wondered out loud. She dabbed the material to her face, blotting the small droplets of blood.

'She thought you were attacking me. She's very sensitive.'

And I'm a block of wood! God, he's priceless! 'I was, and no matter what anyone tells you my temper has been wildly exaggerated.' She couldn't help the hint of defensiveness creeping into her voice. The family joke about her left hook had worn pretty thin years ago, and she'd worked really hard to control her more instinctual responses. It wasn't as if she *liked* losing her temper; it made her sick—physically sick afterwards. She was still shaking with reaction.

'Under the circumstances I'm not going to disagree with you. I'd like to keep my other cheek intact.'

'I've never hit anyone smaller than me.'

'That must certainly reduce your field.'

'That's a cheap crack. I thought you had more class.'

'And you'd know all about class, I suppose?' He moved closer in time to see the flash of anger in her eyes. The absence of colour in her cheeks emphasised the brilliance of their blue. If he'd wanted to he could have counted the number of freckles that were scattered over the bridge of her nose. Make-up on a face like hers really would be a case of gilding the lily. 'And if you're thinking of taking another swing at me, I warn you I'm not into meek acceptance.'

That makes two of us, she thought, narrowing her eyes and lifting her chin. 'I'm sorry I hit you.' The words emerged with the utmost reluctance. 'But you deserved it!' She couldn't prevent the heartfelt postscript. She was proud of the fact she'd tamed her temper, and she didn't like being reminded that at times she could still lose control. 'I haven't hit anyone in...'

'Hours?'

This ironic suggestion made her teeth gouge painful inroads into her full lower lip. 'Years,' she responded with icy dignity. She could still recall the occasion when the stupidity of losing her cool had been brought home to her pretty sharply.

When she and her sisters had come across those yobs threatening to drop the puppy off the bridge into the river, their taunts had made her see red. While she'd been giving the ringleader a bloody nose Anna had been jumping off the bridge into a raging torrent after the puppy and Lindy had been racing downstream to rescue them both. She supposed the incident, which could so easily have ended in tragedy, said quite a lot about their different personalities.

'At least you're ashamed of your latest escapade.'

'Hitting you?' 'Ashamed' was pitching a bit strong.

'Breaking up a marriage.'

'Oh, that,' she said airily. She flicked him a sideways glance—yes, he looked as if he had a particularly unpleasant taste in his mouth. Thinking about his stern mouth made her stomach lurch. It was hard to forget she'd wondered what his lips would feel like, how he'd taste... She willed the flood of warmth that began low in her belly not to spread its heat to her trembling limbs. The last thing she needed right now was her brain to be befuddled by *that* sort of thing!

Well, I'd as soon be hung for a sheep as a lamb, and if he wants a scarlet woman, who am I to disappoint him? One thing she *wasn't* going to be was a penitent sinner who could be redeemed by the marvellous Mr Matheson.

'Lloyd's not a child; he's quite capable of making his own decisions. I think,' she mused thoughtfully, 'you'll find he's very grateful to me.' And he's got reason to be, she silently added.

'Did his wife send you a thank-you card?' He regarded her with fastidious distaste.

'Not exactly.' Hope winced at the memory of her last encounter with Lloyd's famous wife. Dallas had brought along several busloads of the press to record her public humiliation. Apparently the publicity had done the sales of her latest album no harm at all, but Hope didn't imagine she'd receive the credit for that. She chuckled softly at the idea.

'Have you no shame at all?' His face was dark with disgust. 'You find it all a joke?' he asked with incredulous disgust. 'Are you really that self-centred and selfish?'

'Which question shall I answer first?' she puzzled, finger on the small cleft in her chin. 'Or were they all rhetorical?' How was I ever attracted to this man? she wondered. He's narrow-minded and petty! The mocking smile slid from her face, leaving an expression of scornful contempt. 'My conscience is quite clear, thank you, Alex,' she said crisply.

The way his knuckles turned white strangely fascinated her. To look at his face you'd never guess he wants to strangle me, she thought. She was quite familiar with the urge to lash out, but she was confident that he was far too controlled to give in to the impulse to strangle her, or even the one to kiss her. This sudden startling insight made her eyes widen suddenly. The fact that he'd decided she wasn't worthy of his notice didn't stop him from lusting after her. And Alex Matheson was a man who prided himself on being in control of his emotions.

'Do you like playing games with people?' His icy glare impaled her.

'A girl's got to amuse herself.' The nerve in his taut jaw did a triple backflip at that one.

'Is that what you were doing with me?' The flicker in his hooded eyes made Hope feel uneasy, but she wasn't going to back pedal now.

She tilted her head, as if giving the idea serious consideration. It would be a small revenge for the insults Alex Matheson had heaped upon her.

'Well I've got to do *something* for the next month, and I do find *older* men, with that air of authority, so attractive. I'm quite willing to sacrifice youthful stamina for...' she gave a delicate laugh '...competence. I like experienced men,' she confided, with her best come-hither smile. 'But this isn't Hollywood, is it?' she murmured regretfully. 'If you'd been married it wouldn't really have been worth the hassle.'

To think he'd thought her untainted by the life she'd led. To think he'd been enchanted by her open warmth and transparent sincerity! The throbbing in his temples reached new heights. In a different frame of mind Alex would undoubtedly have paused to reflect on the contradictory nature of Hope's responses. But Alex didn't pause; he reached out and grabbed her by the shoulders. He glimpsed shock and dismay in her wide blue eyes before he kissed her.

The pressure of his mouth bent her body back until her head touched the springy moss-covered ground. His hands moved from her shoulders to frame her face, effectively immobilising it. Not that Hope had any thoughts of fighting; she had no thoughts at all. The only information that filtered into her brain concerned simple things, like smell, texture and taste. The smell of the leather gauntlet on his right hand, the wool of his sweater and the citrusy spice of the masculine fragrance he used. The texture of his firm mouth, the sensation as his tongue thrust into the recesses of her mouth and the taste of him... Now she knew. Now she'd never be able to forget it.

It stopped just as suddenly as it had begun. The weak sunlight that his head had blotted out filtered through the transparent thinness of her closed eyelids. She listened to the echo of her own heartbeat.

'Say something,' he said thickly. 'At least look at me.' If he hadn't been able to see her chest rising and falling he wouldn't have known she was alive. Her hair was spread around her face, a rich golden frame. The permanent indentation between his eyes deepened as he stared down at her.

A smile tugged the corners of her mouth. 'How can I refuse an offer like that? Or was it an order? Don't look so surprised, Alex. What did you expect? Hysteria? I've been kissed before...' Not like that, *never* like that. Her nervous system had shut down, unable to accept the messages being fed it. 'Admittedly with more finesse...' To her surprise he perceptibly flinched. He flexed his massive shoulders and his glance slid momentarily from her face.

She was no weakling, but Alex hadn't needed to use more than a fraction of the strength in that awesome upper body to immobilise her. And all the time she'd been aware of the staggering strength he held in check. She hadn't just been aware of it—she'd been deeply excited by it. Alien emotions churned in her belly.

'We're quits,' he observed flatly.

'Given the choice, I'd have taken a slapped face.' A dull red spread over the hard contours of his cheekbones and she felt a surge of satisfaction. 'Though I'm sure you're not the sort of man who'd strike a female.' Her voice was laced with sarcasm.

'I'm sorry I lacked finesse,' he bit back.

Sprawling here, she felt rather vulnerable, but she didn't want to risk moving until she had full control over her limbs again. 'It was a bit naive of me to expect subtlety from someone like you. I don't expect imagination is your strong point—' With a yelp of alarm she closed her eyes. He moved with amazing fluidity for someone of his build.

When she risked opening one eye he was kneeling beside her. The muscles of her abdomen clenched in anticipation of sitting upright. They relaxed instantaneously as he ran the tip of one callused forefinger experimentally down the side of her cheek. Each microscopic downy hair on her smooth skin danced in response. A sound escaped her lips as the air fled from her lungs in one gasp.

'I never did know when to stop,' she croaked. 'I'm sure you're as subtle as hell.'

'For an elderly male with limited reserves of stamina?' he suggested silkily.

'Can't you take a joke?' He was removing the thick padded gauntlet from his hand. A girl who got turned on by looking at a man's hands was in serious trouble, she reflected wildly.

'Creativity takes many shapes and forms.' He lowered himself on one elbow and brushed the tangled curls from her brow. 'I may be colour-blind…'

'How fascinating,' she replied in a high-pitched voice. 'Colour-blind.' He'd tugged the zip of her waterproof jacket far enough down to give his mouth access to the base of her throat. 'This is silly.'

Her words emerged as a breathy gasp rather than a sharp reprimand. She dug her fingers into his rich pelt of hair in order to jerk his head away, but the warm lash of his tongue against the pulse-spot made her fingers curl against his scalp in a manner more intended to hold him against her than repel him.

The open-mouthed assaults on her neck tore a series of soft, guttural moans from Hope's throat. Alex lowered his body as he moved higher, until by the time he was at eye level with her they lay thigh to thigh, chest to chest on the sloping ground.

'It must be difficult for someone used to delicate refinement to be exposed to such crude clumsiness.' The rasp of his voice was close to her ear. His lips grazed the same orifice and sent electrical tremors down to the tip of her curling toes.

Her blue eyes were swimming as she met his hard gaze; her stare was hazy and unfocused. This was torture; each soft, arousing salute was agony. How could so little make her crave so much? He hadn't even touched her body, but she was pierced by a desire so intense she could hardly breathe.

Handicapped by inarticulate frustration and raw need, her first move in response wasn't loaded with finesse. She raised her head a little, dug her fingers hard into his scalp and pressed her lips, chastely closed, to his mouth.

She was breathing fast and hard when she lifted her mouth from his. Grey eyes clashed with blue.

'I want...' Emotion clogged her throat.

'A bit of rough?' The suggestion was as hard as the calculating expression in his eyes.

For a second she couldn't believe what she'd heard. Being plunged into ice was remarkably sobering. She bit down on her lower lip to stop the hurt cry escaping the confines of her throat. She drew her knees protectively up to her chest and rolled over onto her side. Though her knees were shaking, she managed to get to her feet gracefully.

If she'd looked back he'd have been able to see the tears streaming unchecked down her cheeks, so she didn't look back.

'She's invited *who*?'

Beth Lacey didn't appear to notice her daughter's horrified expression.

'Alex Matheson, dear, to make up the numbers. Mind you, he and Adam get on quite well, I believe. They play tennis together, you know.'

'I didn't know,' Hope replied faintly.

'I did mention to Anna that you and he got on really well at the wedding. Shall I do a lemon tart, or be really naughty and risk the chocolate meringue?' She waited expectantly and gave an impatient sigh when her daughter regarded her blankly. 'I told you, we're bringing the pudding. Anna's got enough on her hands without entertaining, but you know Anna, once she's made up her mind. At least she's limiting it to family—and Alex, of course.'

And Alex!

Hope nodded. She knew Anna. She knew Anna well enough to know she couldn't ask her to retract the invitation to Alex without having the whole humiliating tale exposed. Hope wasn't ready for that; she was still feeling far too raw about the whole painful incident. There was only one thing for it.

'Sorry, Mum, I've got to go out,' she said, levering her tall frame from the saggy armchair.

'Where to?'

Hand on the doorhandle, Hope smiled vaguely. 'I won't be long. I'll borrow your car.'

It took her less time than it ought to reach Matheson Motors on the edge of the small market town. She parked her mother's old banger amongst less rusty cars and walked confidently up to the entrance. No one watching her long-legged elegant stride could have guessed how close to open panic she was. Only her sisters knew that she only whistled when she was petrified, and they weren't here.

The girl in Reception looked up and visibly did a double take. 'Miss Lacey,' she gasped, her eyes widening. 'Can I help you?' she added hopefully, regaining some of her professional poise.

'I'd like to see Alex.' A famous face did have some compensations, especially when you wanted to bluff your way into somewhere you had no right to be.

'Mr Matheson...' Doubt crossed the other girl's face. 'Do you have an appointment?'

'It's a surprise.'

'Well, I don't think... He's quite strict about...'

'Actually,' Hope said, leaning forward in a confidential manner, 'I'm meant to be having dinner with him tonight, but I'm going to have to cry off. So I thought I'd take him for an early lunch to compensate.'

'For his birthday? I see. Oh, well, in that case...'

Alex's PA turned out to be male, quite a young, attractive male, who wasn't totally immune to her charms. She'd have liked to think it was her famous smile and winning manner that had allowed her to enter the inner sanctum which he so jealously guarded, but it was obvious she'd only got this far because Alex had given his permission.

Panic closed in as the door shut behind her. Pride made it imperative that she didn't show her uncertainty.

She needn't have worried; for all the interest Alex showed in her she might as well have been standing there stark naked. She couldn't have felt more vulnerable if she had been!

He continued to peel off a set of navy overalls, underneath which he wore a pristine white shirt and silk tie. He lifted the dark grey jacket missing from his ensemble from the back of his chair and slipped it on. The shadow of body hair was visible through the thin fabric of his shirt, as was the suggestion of musculature. Hope's throat grew painfully dry as she tried not to notice these facts.

'You've got a hands-on management style, I see,' she said, her eyes flicking to the discarded utilitarian overalls.

'I'm a hands-on sort of guy.'

The innuendo made the colour flare in her cheeks. 'I expect you know why I'm here.'

'I'm not nearly so perceptive as you appear to think.'

'The dinner party.' She didn't want to play games with him. She wasn't capable of playing games with him. Just being in the same room as him was making her aware of how deeply he'd managed to unnerve her.

'Ah, the dinner party.' He lowered himself into the deeply padded leather swivel chair behind the massive desk which dominated the room. No, she mentally corrected herself, it was Alex who dominated the room— this room and any other room he was in.

'Don't go.'

'Pardon? I'm forgetting my manners—won't you have a seat?'

'You can't forget what you've never had,' she snapped back. 'And I'm not staying long enough to sit down. Don't think I enjoy being in your company.'

'If that is so, why you here?' he enquired imperturbably. He watched her with a narrow-eyed silver stare that made her shiver.

'I just wanted to ask you to be reasonable. I'm sure you don't want to spend an evening in my company any more than I want to spend an evening in yours.'

'If you didn't want to see me, why come here?'

'I've already told you—'

'Ever heard of the telephone?' he interrupted cryptically.

Hope's mouth opened and closed several times before her voice returned. 'I didn't think of that.'

'Of course you didn't...' he drawled.

The hateful *knowing* look in his eyes made her want to scream. 'If you think I used this as a pretext to see you,' she returned scornfully, 'you couldn't be more wrong!'

'Now there's an interesting idea,' he mused, resting his chin on his steepled fingers.

She couldn't look at his hands without imagining... Hope took a deep, steadying breath. I will not lose my temper, she repeated slowly to herself. I won't! 'Are you going to come?' She sounded calm and reasonable.

'I could hardly refuse after they've asked me to be godfather to little Joe.'

'They haven't.' She closed her eyes and pushed back the wing of hair that flopped in her eyes. 'They've asked me to be his godmother.'

'Isn't that nice?' His teeth were as white and even as your average wolf's.

'You're enjoying this!' she accused.

For the first time he looked less than indolent as his body stiffened in the chair. 'Far from it,' he snapped. 'But I'm not going to offend friends just because they have the misfortune to be related to a shallow little trollop like you! Sorry,' he corrected, looking her up and down slowly, 'cancel the "little"...'

'I'm wasting my time here.' She turned on her heel and strode from the office. 'How do I get out of here?' she asked the surprised-looking PA.

'First left and take the lift. If you're in a hurry...?'

'I am.'

'You could go through the factory floor, turn right and down the stairs.'

Hope was blind to the eyes that followed her across

the factory floor. Matheson cars were strictly low-tech, at least as far as their construction went, so there was no robot technology—just a dedicated, highly trained workforce. She didn't even register the warning cry as the ground disappeared beneath her.

At moments like this a girl with any sense would faint, she thought. Hope waited for the blackness to enfold her and block out the excruciating pain, but it didn't. Someone flicked a switch and the inspection pit was illuminated by brilliant light. Hope showed extreme restraint and moaned softly in reply to several anxious enquiries.

'Get the boss.'

Get an ambulance, she wanted to scream. Instead she fainted, for the first time in her life.

CHAPTER THREE

'DON'T touch her,' She heard an authoritative voice grate.

To Hope, this sounded like excellent advice. The pain seemed to be everywhere, but the moment she tried to move it had been obvious the worst damage had been done to her left leg.

'We thought we ought to give her the kiss of life.'

'Or put her in the recovery position,' another voice added.

'For God's sake, man, she's breathing. She's just fainted, and from the angle of that leg it's just as well.' The brusque reply was much closer this time. 'Where's that ambulance?'

'I don't faint.' She felt impelled to protest this point.

'She's awake; she said something.'

'What is it, Hope?' The touch on her forehead was firm but gentle, and she could smell Alex's distinctive cologne mingled with the warm, musky scent of his body.

'I didn't faint.' She forced her eyes open and found his face very close.

'That's too bad. I expect it's hurting like hell.'

'My leg?'

'It looks broken,' he told her matter-of-factly. 'Where else does it hurt?'

'Everywhere.' Weak tears started to seep from her eyes and she felt ashamed. 'I'm meant to be modelling swimwear in the Maldives next month.' A spurt of hysterical laughter followed this admission.

'The ambulance won't be long. Just hold on.' She sensed rather than saw him move away. Agitation made her move restlessly. 'Don't try to move, Hope.'

'Promise you won't go away,' she whispered fiercely. Her eyes were glittering feverishly as she caught his hand in a surprisingly strong grip.

A flicker of something close to shock crossed Alex's face. He froze, and his eyes dwelt momentarily on her tightly clenched fingers before moving to her face. 'I promise.' Hope gave a sigh and relaxed.

When the paramedics arrived she was forced to relinquish her hold on Alex's arm. The loss of contact made her come close to losing her tenuous control.

'She needs something for the pain,' she heard him say harshly.

'Don't worry, sir. We won't move her until that's sorted.'

Too right you won't, mate, Hope thought, trying to bring the bewildering scene into focus. This being brave business was not all it was cracked up to be. She made sudden contact with a pair of familiar grey eyes. Something in the calmness of his gaze must have transmitted itself to her, because it was suddenly a lot easier to follow the paramedic's instructions to grip the mask and breathe in the gas and air mixture. This almost instantaneously took the edge off the pain. It didn't disappear, but it was easier to cope with.

Someone stuck an injection in her thigh before her leg was cocooned in a splint and she was strapped to a stretcher.

'Are you coming with us, sir?'

Hope pulled the mask off her face. 'You don't have to.' Alex bent his head closer to catch her words and she repeated herself.

'I'll come.' Hope closed her eyes and gave a small,

satisfied smile. Why she should feel safer knowing he was within grabbing distance was a mystery she would unravel at a later date.

'How are you feeling?' Alex raised his voice against the noise of the siren. Dear God, man, he thought with savage impatience, why not simply talk about the weather? That would be almost as inane! He functioned well in a crisis, but once command of the situation had been taken out of his hands he felt frustratingly impotent.

'Drunk,' came back the surprising reply.

Alex looked questioningly to the paramedic. 'It's the drugs and the gas and air. It affects some people that way.'

'Do you know something?'

'What, Hope?'

'You've got the most beautiful hands I've ever seen,' she confided in a slurred tone.

'That's very kind of you to say so.'

'I wanted to say so. Something else I wanted to tell you, Alex—' she began.

Alex turned and the paramedic swiftly smothered the smirk on his face. 'I think we might discuss this later on, Hope.'

'I've forgotten what it was anyway.'

'Well, aren't you a lucky girl?'

Was she meant to reply to that one? Hope wondered. Wearing a white coat seemed to endow its owner with an endless supply of platitudes.

'We'll whip you up to Theatre shortly, and realign that tibia, and you'll be as good as new in next to no time. The ribs will be sore for a while, but they're only cracked. You're really very...'

'If you tell me one more time how lucky I am, Adam,

so help me I'll realign your nose,' she said wearily, but with sincerity.

Her brother-in-law cast a dampening glare at his tittering minions. 'Someone who throws herself into pits and doesn't break her neck has to expect clichés, Hope.'

Her grin was a shadow of its former self. 'Has anyone told Mum and Dad yet?' she asked fretfully.

'Alex insisted on doing that personally. He thought it would give them less anxiety than a phone call.'

'I see.' So that was where he'd gone. Since she'd been placed in the care of her brother-in-law she hadn't seen him. She did have an embarrassing recollection of clinging tenaciously to his hand, but details were rather hazy. 'What's that she's got?' she asked suspiciously as a nurse materialised at the bedside.

'A pre-med, Hope, to calm you down.'

'I am calm. Any more calm and I'd—'

'Why don't you shut up, Hope, and let us do our job? If you'd prefer another doctor you're entitled...'

'We've been through all that, Adam, and I'm quite happy with you so long as your precious ethics don't get in the way of treating a family member.'

'Oh, my ethics can take the strain. It's the nursing staff I'm worried about.'

Hope was still grumbling quietly to herself when she drifted once more into a drug-induced slumber.

Three days later she was packing up her belongings—or at least giving instructions whilst her mother did so for her.

'Lovely flowers, dear,' her mother observed, fondly regarding the large bouquet of yellow roses arranged in a tall vase.

'Send them to the children's ward,' Hope put in quickly.

'Quite sure?'

Hope smiled grimly. Her mother wasn't going to find a card no matter how hard she looked, because she had removed it—ripped it up and thrown it away with the other rubbish. There had been just one word on the card; *Alex,* written in a bold, strong hand.

She'd woken up the previous afternoon to find him standing there beside her bed, holding the roses. It must have been raining outside because his hair had been wetly slicked back, curling slightly over the collar of his leather jacket. A film of moisture had covered the faintly tanned olive-toned skin of his face, enhancing the air of healthy vitality he exuded.

Her eyes had skimmed over the sharp planes of his face, touched the firm lines of his sexy mouth before coming to rest on his eyes—eyes that followed the slanting line of his dark eyebrows, eyes that were silver-flecked grey and, most significantly, eyes that sent an electrical surge spiralling through her body. She'd felt stunned; she hadn't dreamed this feeling, it had really happened. She'd felt restless, weak and excited all at the same time.

'Thank you. They look beautiful,' she'd said shyly.

Shyness wasn't an emotion Hope was accustomed to and it made her feel awkward. His keen eyes were missing no details of her ravaged face. 'It looks worse than it is.' She spoke self-consciously.

Though, spectacular and painful, the bruising which covered most of the left side of her body would leave no lasting damage. She wasn't vain, but she wanted him to see her at her best, which in all modesty she knew was a pretty good best. Instead she looked like something out of a horror film. Sod's law! she thought fatalistically.

'I wouldn't have thought it was in your best interests to admit that.'

Confusion settled on her face. Her brain still felt a bit like cotton wool. Had she missed a complete segment of conversation here? What did he mean? Or was he implying she ought to enjoy being a patient? If that was so she could swiftly disillusion him on that score!

'Don't worry.' He forestalled her reply. 'I didn't come here to discuss that.'

'Discuss—?'

He silenced her with an imperative hand. 'I understand your position completely.'

I wish *I* did! Hope's confusion deepened; this grave comment didn't have the ring of sympathetic empathy to it.

'I wanted to see for myself how you are. There are *no* ulterior motives, Hope. I hope you understand that.'

Hope managed to keep her expression neutral, but it took a phenomenal effort. The minute she'd opened her eyes and seen him standing there she'd known—and it seemed he did too. The hazy dream-like recollections of the time immediately following the accident probably told only part of the story. God knows what I did, she thought, humiliation washing over her. God knows what I said.

'I didn't want there to be any misunderstandings.'

Hope cleared her throat, which still felt a little raw after the anaesthetic. 'I appreciate that,' she said. His clinical regard sharpened, grew less impersonal as he absorbed the husky catch in her voice. Hope didn't flinch from his regard and he was the first to look away. She was glad. I've done nothing to be ashamed of, she decided rebelliously. Falling in love was no crime, even when the recipient of those feelings was as reluctant as Alex obviously was.

Privately she thought there was a big difference between blunt and brutal. What does he think? she wondered. That I'm going to fling myself at him and declare my undying passion? It hurt to know he wasn't prepared to risk it.

He hadn't even said goodbye... The sound of her mother's voice pulled her out of her gloomy reverie.

'I'll take them along to the nurses' station, shall I?' Beth Lacey repeated, with an expression of regret.

Hope wasn't left alone long before her brother-in-law put his head around the door; the rest of his lean body swiftly followed suit.

'All set, then?'

'Thankfully, yes.'

'You're a terrible patient.'

'Says you,' she replied disrespectfully.

'Seen Alex lately?'

Hope stiffened at this seemingly casual question. 'Why should I have seen Alex?'

Adam flicked her a curious but not unkind look. 'You were screaming at the top of your lungs for him when you came out of the anaesthetic.'

'There are a lot of Alexes in the world.' Is there no escape from the man? I can't even be unconscious in peace!

'Thousands.'

'If you mention this to anyone I'll...' People did things that were totally out of character when under the influence—bizarre things. Things that had no significance. Her mental protestations offered little comfort.

'Don't worry, it's covered by patient confidentiality.' Adam gave his stethoscope a casual twirl.

'By anyone I especially mean Anna.'

Adam grinned, but didn't respond to this challenge.

'Duty calls,' he said, moving purposefully towards the door. 'Good man, Alex Matheson. I like him.'

If I wasn't stuck in this damned thing, she thought, banging the sides of her wheelchair, I wouldn't let him get away with that. Damn that man, she fumed, and it wasn't Adam she was referring to.

'We'll postpone the trip.'

Hope wheeled around awkwardly on the crutches. 'Don't you dare!' Her parents had been planning their world cruise for over a year now, and they'd been talking about it for as long as she could remember. She couldn't bear being the cause of them missing their dream holiday. 'I'm quite capable of coping.'

'I'd only worry about you, dear. If Anna didn't have her hands full with the babies you could go there...'

'I don't need anyone to look after me. I've only got a plaster on my leg, Mum.' It was frustrating to know she was fighting a losing battle. Once her mother made up her mind there was no unmaking it. She silently cursed overdeveloped maternal instincts.

'There's the door,' Beth said, levering herself up from her armchair at the sound of a strident peal on the doorbell. It occurred to Hope, not for the first time in the past two weeks, that for once her mother was looking her age—she needed this holiday; she worked far too hard.

'I'll get it,' Hope responded, gritting her teeth in a determined fashion as she did a neat three-point turn to get through the doorway. She balanced on one leg to open the front door before clutching once more at her crutches. 'It's you.' She immediately flushed under the ironic stare she received in return. Of all the *stupid* things to say!

'You're looking well.' The purple bruises that had

decorated one side of her face, and other areas not on public display, had faded to pale yellow patches in the two weeks since the accident. His eyes narrowed slightly as he examined the visible evidence of her fall.

His deep voice did the most insane things to her metabolism. 'I'm fine, just fine. Won't you come in?' She'd forgotten just how intimidating his physical presence could be. Her eyes ran furtively over the strong, muscular lines of his shoulders and she cleared her throat noisily. 'Please come in. Nice weather, lovely day...' She managed to stop the irritating flow of banalities.

'If it's not inconvenient.' The only reaction he made to the parrot-like style of her conversation was a slight inclination of one darkly defined eyebrow.

Nice weather, lovely day—inwardly she groaned as she felt the rivulets of sweat trickle down her spine. It had only stopped snowing half an hour ago, and the driving conditions were appalling. What's wrong with me? Pull yourself together, girl!

'I know you don't want to see me.' His dark, sombre face was impossible to read.

'I don't?' She was treading warily. There was transference if ever she'd heard it, she thought sourly. It must be something urgent to make him voluntarily seek her out. He was probably going to warn her not to stalk him!

'But my lawyer couldn't contact your agent today, and there are a few details that need to be sorted out without delay...'

She was totally at sea. 'Jonathan?'

'Jonathan Harkness *is* your agent, isn't he?' Impatience was evident in his tone.

'Well, I've only got one.' And sometimes he was more trouble than he was worth. Jonathan's agenda for her career and her own could diverge pretty dramatically at times.

'I know you don't want to get involved personally, but—'

'Can we just stop there?' she interrupted. 'It's not very comfortable for me standing for too long.' She glanced pointedly at her plaster-encased leg. 'Come along to the sitting room.'

'Alex, how lovely to see you. I'll go and get some tea, shall I?' Beth said to nobody in particular before she disappeared.

Subtle as a sledgehammer, thought Hope, left with a strained smile on her face. 'Perhaps you'd better tell me what's brought you here.' Since it wasn't the charm of my personality, she added silently. She avoided the arm-chair—once she got down there it was difficult to get back up. Instead she sat in a oak ladder-backed chair with a sagging rush seat.

'The fact that I'm perfectly ready to accept responsibility was meant to facilitate a speedy conclusion to this affair. However, your legal people appear to take that as a sign of weakness.' He began to pace the room. He moved softly for a big man. His anger was evident in the rigidity of his straight spine. 'The demands they're making now are absurd by anyone's reckoning. This last fax I got...' he began, his voice like subdued thunder.

He abruptly pulled a rumpled sheet of paper from his pocket and crushed it in one strong hand, before flinging it savagely onto the floor. 'You've picked on the wrong man if you want a fight, Hope. I won't be manipulated. I'll accept responsibility, but I won't lie down for anyone to walk over me.'

'Alex,' she said quietly, 'I don't know what you're talking about.' There was no mistaking the menace he was emanating, but the cause was a total mystery to her. Anger began to supplant her confusion. She'd done nothing to deserve being on the receiving end of his threats.

'Do you mean to tell me you *didn't* tell Harkness not to accept my offer?' He regarded her with scornful disbelief.

'I don't even know why you should know Jonathan,' she said firmly. 'If you're going to look at me as though I'm something nasty and slimy underfoot, I'd at least like to know what I'm meant to have done!'

His eyes searched her face. 'You're serious, aren't you?' he said slowly. 'You really don't know what I'm talking about.' He shook his head in disbelief and sank into an armchair. He was a big man and he looked to be firmly wedged in the floral-patterned chair.

'You might need a crane to get you out of there.' From out of the blue her devilish sense of humour resurfaced.

The smile slipped slowly from her face as her eyes dwelt on the muscled contours of his thighs, moulded by the denim of his black jeans. How would it feel to touch...? The steamy graphic flow of speculation was debilitating. Her body felt as if it had been abruptly isolated from her energy supply. If she hadn't been sitting she'd have fallen.

Good God, this had to stop! She'd always thought people who acted crazy when they fell in love were slightly pitiful. 'If the man's a monster or he doesn't love you go look for someone else,' she'd told friends on numerous occasions—it had all seemed so simple then. What she hadn't understood then was that love wasn't pliable at all; it was the poor sucker who'd succumbed that did all the bending.

'Harkness approached me the day after the accident—'

'You still don't believe that I know nothing about it, do you?' she interrupted, bristling with antagonism. The resignation in his voice made it clear to her he was going through the motions; he couldn't actually bring himself to believe she was as ignorant as she claimed.

'You've got to admit that it's pretty far-fetched. Why would your agent keep you in the dark?'

Jon was developing a nasty habit of doing just that lately, she reflected grimly. If he suspected she wasn't going to follow his advice he left it to the last minute to discuss things with her—when, of course, it was more difficult for her to say no. She was going to have some very hard words with Jonathan.

'Well, I'll just have to feign shock when you tell me what you two have been hatching, won't I?' Her voice was bitingly sarcastic.

Alex inclined his head and went so far as to allow a faint smile to play fleetingly across his lips. 'He pointed out, quite correctly, that legally I was responsible for your accident. He also told me how much money you were going to lose because you were unable to fulfil your commitments.'

Hope's mind was racing. This was the third and final year of the lucrative swimwear contract. She knew there was a penalty clause if she was unable to complete her contract. All the same, Jonathan had had no right!

'Don't worry,' she said grimly, 'I don't want your money!' Wait until she saw Jon again. How *dare* he place her in this position? And how dared Alex assume that she was party to it?

'That's hardly a practical stand to take, Hope. I was quite prepared to make restitution—I still am. It was just the new figure which they've now come up with I object to.'

'How much?' she asked abruptly. The sum he mentioned made her grow pale with anger. Her anger, which had been firmly aimed at her absent agent suddenly shifted direction. 'You thought I was party to that sort of…of *extortion!*'

'It's legal when lawyers do it, Hope.'

'I don't care if it's legal or not,' she fumed, 'I don't want your money.'

'I wouldn't be too hasty if I were you…' he drawled. Her antagonism was more convincing than anything she'd said.

'You're not,' she snapped, 'and neither is Jonathan. And I don't need either of you to tell me what I need or want. That's what you were talking about in the hospital,' she said suddenly, her eyes flying wide open. 'I thought…'

'What did you think?'

She threw him a startled glance, which swiftly grew belligerent. 'None of your damned business.' It was worse, really. At least before she'd thought he was telling her he wasn't attracted to her. She supposed this was the only logical next step as far as he was concerned… *I'm perfectly happy to break up a happy home so why stop there?* An avaricious money-grubber who is determined to make a profit at all costs was an easy progression.

'I don't know why you're getting so emotional about this.'

'Emotional?' she repeated in a low, dangerous tone. 'Emotional!' Her voice soared effortlessly up the scale. 'Don't you dare patronise me, Alex Matheson!'

'I'm in the middle of some sensitive negotiations at the moment, and I don't want any bad publicity, Hope,' he said frankly. 'I'd like this business concluded swiftly. I'm quite happy to pay for any distress and inconvenience you might have suffered. It's not as if we're friends—this is business.'

She stared at him, her bosom heaving with emotion.

That puts me firmly in my place, doesn't it? How, she wondered, could *anyone* be so insensitive? 'Might? There's no *might* about it. You haven't got enough money to compensate me for the distress you've caused.' For the moment she didn't care what interpretation he put on her words. 'You haven't got enough money to compensate me for being in the same room as you.'

Her temper dissipated abruptly, leaving misery in its place. He didn't want any bad publicity for his precious company. There was no genuine concern for her—he didn't care. But then why should he? she reminded herself. She heaved herself to her feet and he slowly followed suit.

'Tell your mother I couldn't stop for tea.'

'She'll be devastated,' she responded childishly.

Mother wasn't coming back. Hope had realised that some time ago. No doubt she thought she was being tactful. Pity it wasn't Dad who was home; he would have watched over her like a mother hen.

'I suggest you don't make any decisions while you're in this mood. You might regret them later. This isn't pennies we're talking here.'

She gritted her teeth. 'Nothing would give me greater pleasure than to drag you through the courts.'

'That's what I like to see—a consistent attitude.' The amusement in his voice was insultingly indulgent.

'I'd like to punch you, too, but I'm not going to.'

'This display of maturity is stunning.'

She tossed her head and her lips compressed in an obstinate line. She wasn't going to let that sly, sarcastic drawl rile her. She could be the soul of restraint when she wanted to be.

'Incidentally, the men—the ones you were just consigning to redundancy—send their best wishes. You had them quite worried.'

He really liked to turn the screws—the rat!

It was only a wobble, and she'd have been perfectly able to steady herself if Alex hadn't chosen to wade in and get all macho and physical.

The arm that snaked around her waist lifted both legs—the injured and sound one—clear off the ground. She wasn't a small girl, and the fact he could do this with no apparent effort was impressive.

Breathless, she found herself clamped against his chest. The man was solid as oak and just as hard. Hope wasn't the sort of girl who'd ever been impressed by well-developed biceps, but Alex hit her at a level she'd never experienced before. The urge to cling and melt against him was staggering.

'My ribs were only cracked, and I'd like to keep it that way,' she croaked. She had to do something before she made a total fool of herself.

It was rare that Alex forgot his strength and didn't adjust his actions accordingly. His apology was brusque and barely audible. She missed the unusual sight of his heightened colour because his face was averted from her as he placed her carefully back on her feet. She grasped a chair-back and he bent down to pick up her fallen crutches.

He got to eye level with her thigh, and no farther. He didn't need to reach out and touch, he didn't want to, but he did. Just looking at the smooth curve of her calf made his belly muscles tighten viciously. The long, lovely line of her thigh made the blood in his temples pound. Fantasies were one thing—this was altogether more dangerous. The fascination defied logic; it was a visceral gut response.

Hope gasped. His fingers could easily span the curve of her uninjured calf. She stopped breathing as hand over hand, fingers splayed to cover a wide area, he worked his way higher. The sensuality of the slow progress instantly sent a flood of intense heat through her body. Her flesh tingled where the fine denier fabric of her stocking chafed her skin. A voice, unheeded, told her she ought to stop the marauding fingers which instigated the sinful friction, but she didn't.

Alex was almost as shocked by his action as she was. A wave of self-contempt swept over him. Damn it, man, talk your way out of this one without looking like a drooling idiot! There was no way he could write this off as accidental.

The muscles of his own thighs tensed and bunched as he began to rise, and his fingertips inadvertently moved above the lacy band at the top of the hold-up stocking she wore on her uninjured leg. Her skin was warm and silkily smooth. Shockingly he could sense through his fingertips the ripple that quivered through the inner muscles of her thigh at his touch. His eyes darkened and he rose to his feet abruptly. The short kick-pleated skirt she wore proved no obstacle to his big hands. They curved firmly over the smooth contours of her rounded behind.

Her head had fallen back and Alex could see the muscles in her extended neck, taut and tense. The tension in her body transmitted itself in tiny intermittent tremors. She was breathing deep and heavily. Her intense sensitivity filled him with a gloating delight. When he transferred one hand to the back of her head and forced her face up to him she looked directly back at him.

For a long, silent moment they looked at one another. Hope could smell the heat of his arousal. Being securely locked hip to hip against the pulsing betrayal of his desire was more darkly exciting than anything she'd ever known. The skin was pulled tightly over the sharp planes of his face and a faint sheen of sweat made it shine. She blinked away the momentary image of a predatory hawk dropping upon its prey.

Whatever else she was going to do she *had* to kiss him. She did. She took his face between her hands and pressed her lips carefully to his. What began as exploratory swiftly became something quite different. His tongue was no longer passive as it suggestively probed the moist warmness of her mouth. His lips ground fiercely against hers with a hunger which awakened an answering fervour within her.

Half lifting her, he moved until her back was pressing into the wall. His hips ground rhythmically against her lower body, driving her half insane with desire.

He drew away, breathing hard. Fist clenched, he rubbed his knuckles delicately over her parted lips. Hope kissed what he offered, a languorous rapture still filling her eyes.

Alex audibly gasped before unclenching his fingers and capturing the curve of her jaw in his hand. 'You are altogether unbelievable,' he said throatily. 'Under the circumstances I can't blame him.'

Confusion crept into her eyes as she turned her cheek into the palm of his hand.

'Any man would be likely to forget he was married when you turn up the heat. In your position the temptation to use your God-given gifts must be irresistible.'

Lloyd—he was talking about Lloyd. The realisation seared through her body. Her hand came up to his shoulders and she pushed, even though she knew her efforts would have no impact on him.

'Let me go!' she breathed, through clenched teeth. Her wild movement sent a watercolour that was hung just above her head crashing to the floor. Shards of wood and gold leaf from the frame scattered over the carpet. Amazingly, the glass stayed intact.

The noise seemed to recall Alex to his surroundings. The quiet, chintzy normality of the room seemed a million miles away from... He lifted his hands abruptly from her, looked with a stunned expression at the palms and then back at Hope's flushed face. His hands fell to his sides.

'You're right. This isn't the time or place,' he said abruptly.

Hope felt sick. He still thought she was a slut—just a desirable slut! 'There isn't a right time or place. Not for you.' Chin up, she prepared to withstand whatever he chose to throw at her.

'I'm not a fool, Hope, I know when a woman wants me.' With a dismissive, half-impatient gesture, Alex thrust his fingers through his hair.

'I have to look beyond basic desire.' She gave a shrug. 'I have to look ahead. Lloyd could give my career in films a kick-start. What can you give me? You have to look at this from my point of view.' At least he looked shocked; that was something. Why look shocked? she wanted to ask. If I was the woman you think I am, isn't that what I'd be thinking?

'Are you asking me to believe that you're no better than a high-class hooker?'

'I'm not asking you to believe that, Alex, that's what you *do* believe,' she pointed out gravely. 'I don't want anything to do with you while that's the case.'

'You want me to believe that half the world's press got it wrong? That's a lot of doubt to give anyone the benefit of. Why not just be honest? There's nobody here but us. I can appreciate you want to shield your parents from the truth, and I'm sure they find your fairy tales comforting, but spare me.'

'I wasn't about to defend myself to you.'

'That's convenient, because I'm not a gullible parent

who wants to believe the lines I'm being fed. Listen, Hope, I admit that initially I thought you were something you're not. I'm not saying you misled me intentionally...'

'That's big of you.'

'It was pretty naive of me, considering the sort of circles you've been moving in since your teens. I don't expect a girl survives without developing a hard skin. It's nothing to do with me who you've slept with or why.'

What a nice, open-minded, tolerant creature he was, she thought, watching him from under the sweep of her lashes. Where was all this leading to? she wondered grimly.

'You must be finding it pretty constricting, being stuck here?'

'I must?'

'I don't have any illusions for you to shatter.'

'I'll sleep better knowing that.'

'With me, I hope,' he said smoothly, ignoring the sarcasm in her tone. 'It's what we both want and you've not a lot else to do.'

Old-fashioned courting. There was nothing quite like it. 'I can quite honestly say,' she said, her voice trembling with suppressed emotion, 'that I've never had a proposition quite like that before.'

'I like to be original.' He didn't appear to be waiting with bated breath for her reply. He looked quietly confident and insultingly casual about the entire thing.

'Pacifism,' she said unsteadily, 'is suddenly looking much less appealing.' Tears of sheer fury were stinging the back of her eyelids.

'Dear God, woman, is it *that* important for you to preserve your wholesome nice-girl role?'

'I *am* a nice girl, but if you don't leave immediately

I'll forget the fact and tell you exactly what I think of you.'

His square jaw tightened, but he smiled with unique unpleasantness. 'Have it your way. But you might regret this noble stance when you're lying alone in your virginal white sheets.'

'I hope thinking of my virginal sheets gives you a good night's sleep!' She flung the words at his broad back.

Hope had no way of knowing that this dart had accurately found its target—Alex's back was not very revealing.

CHAPTER FOUR

'WELL, what's this brilliant idea of yours, then?' Hope asked her sister, who invaded rather than visited these days. It was bewildering, she reflected, just how much paraphernalia two small babies required.

'Here, hold your godson,' Anna said, extracting one of her sons from the Moses basket. 'Support his head.'

Easy for you to say, Hope thought as she obediently received the soft bundle on her lap. 'I'm not very good with babies,' she replied uncertainly. The tiny creature in her arms stared back placidly at her with the unnerving intensity of a new-born. 'Hello, shrimp,' she said softly. A tiny fist closed around her probing finger and she gasped. 'He's so strong.'

Anna gave a small complacent smile. 'He's superior to other babies in every way,' she agreed. 'So is Henry.' She surreptitiously glanced at the sleeping infant in the vacated crib. 'Speaking of whom, do you mind keeping your voice down? He's not nearly so quiet as Joe when he's awake.'

'You were talking about your brilliant idea...' Hope cast the sleeping figure a suspicious look. Faced with a crying baby, she suspected she might well panic. Glancing at the contented face of her sister, she wondered where Anna had learnt what to do. Did it really come naturally? Perhaps there's some essential mothering factor missing in me, she pondered.

'I've worked out a way to make Mum and Dad go on their cruise.'

'That's marvellous!' Despite the cheerful face their

mother had been putting on, Hope knew how much both her parents had been looking forward to the trip.

'We'll work out a rota.'

'Rota?'

'A "make sure poor helpless Hope isn't in trouble" rota. A "make sure she's fed and washed" rota.'

Hope looked doubtful. 'That doesn't sound very practical to me. You've got your hands full…and it's not as if you're right on the doorstep.'

'I know, I know,' said Anna impatiently. 'I've decided to delegate.'

Hope frowned. She suspected she wasn't going to like the sound of this. 'How, exactly?'

'Well, I can pop over every other afternoon and spend an hour with you before I pick up Sam and Nathan from nursery school, and on alternate days you can get a taxi up to our place, so there's no possibility of you being lonely. Adam will come in every morning to check you didn't die in the night, and the Wilsons will be around the farm all day—so if you scream loud enough they'll be bound to hear…'

'I'm not helpless.' Hope had to smile at Anna's enthusiasm.

'I know that, but it's Mum we have to convince. As I was saying, you can promise to carry the mobile with you everywhere, and Alex will pop in every night.'

'What?'

'Hush, you'll wake Henry,' Anna said reproachfully. She glanced quickly at her son to satisfy herself he was still asleep. 'Cherub,' she said fondly, before turning her attention back to her sister. 'Alex has kindly agreed to look in every night. I'd get Adam to do it, but to be honest I need him myself just now.'

'You're mad if you think Alex Matheson will play nursemaid.'

This had to be a nightmare! She had to do some quick talking. If Anna got her way—her mind refused to explore this humiliating avenue.

She couldn't tell Anna the truth. Anna didn't know the meaning of subtlety, and she was quite capable of marching up to Alex and demanding he explain himself. It was hard enough coping with things as it was—what with her moods dramatically veering from brave optimism to maudlin self-pity. If he *knew!* Hope shuddered at the thought.

'Hardly nursemaid. Anyway,' Anna said with a triumphant smile, 'he was delighted. Well, he didn't say no anyhow. He's got lovely manners.'

'He's managed to hide them from me.'

'Don't tell me you've had a lovers' tiff?' Anna said in an exasperated tone. 'That explains it.'

'Explains it?' Hope said sharply. 'What do you mean, lovers? Has Adam been talking?'

'Adam? You mean he knows? Isn't that just like him,' Anna said, reflecting with a frown on her husband's shortcomings. 'He didn't say a word. Wait till I see him! No, I merely put two and two together. I know you were with Alex at the wedding, because at least three people told me, and you were at his factory when you had your accident. So, unless you've developed an interest in the manufacture of cars... I put two and two together—because you didn't choose to confide in me.'

'There's nothing to confide.'

'Just a string of coincidences—I know. The fact is, Alex dropping in every night will be the clincher with Mum. The farm is pretty isolated. After I pointed out that it was his fault you're in this mess to begin with—'

'Anna, you didn't!' Hope groaned.

'Well, it was his hole you fell down, wasn't it?' her sister replied, with an innocent smile that didn't fool

Hope for an instant. 'I didn't think you'd have any objections about him tucking you in at night,' she observed with a frankly wicked smile. 'I tell you something, Hope, you're a big improvement on the one he brought to our place the other month.'

Hope was instantly diverted. 'Who would that be?' She managed casual interest quite brilliantly. Nobody watching her would have guessed the degree of jealousy this information had given rise to.

'I think she's a banker. I've never seen a banker that looks like her.'

'That's sexist, Anna.'

'No, just spiteful.'

'She's *very* good-looking, then?' Why did I ask? I must have a masochistic streak a mile wide, Hope thought helplessly.

Anna sniffed. 'Too thin,' she replied, wrinkling her nose. 'Looked like she lived on her nerves. Jumped like a cat every time you spoke to her. Anyhow, she's yesterday's news, isn't she?'

'For God's sake, Anna, don't go around telling people that Alex and I are...are...'

'An item?'

'Definitely not,' Hope said firmly. 'He thinks I'm a bimbo.' She was too harassed to come up with anything but the truth.

'You!' Anna burst out laughing. 'Don't be silly.'

Hope could have wept with frustration. 'Seriously.'

Anna stopped laughing and frowned. 'The idiot!' she exclaimed indignantly. 'Wait till I—'

'No!' Hope interrupted firmly. 'You will not, and I repeat, *not* interfere, Anna.'

Anna's dark eyes searched her sister's face, and what she saw there made her expression grow sober. 'He's made you unhappy? That's it, then. Plan cancelled.'

'I did it.'

Both sisters looked up as Adam Deacon entered the room. He looked pleased with himself.

'You did what?' his wife asked suspiciously.

'Persuaded Beth that she could go on the cruise with a clear conscience. I managed to soothe her every fear,' he observed with modest pride. 'Though I think the fact that Alex is going to play guard dog at night really clinched it. I can see her point—you really are a bit off the beaten track here, and he's only two minutes away by car. You should have seen her face. She's so excited, and already planning the packing with military precision.'

'Oh, Adam, how could you?' Anna reproached him.

'What do you mean, how could I?' he said incredulously. 'I didn't volunteer. The way I recall it *you* were the one who said we should take advantage of the fact I'm a smooth talker.'

'That was before,' Anna responded crossly.

'Before what?'

'Don't start, you two,' Hope said forcefully. 'It's done now.' She wasn't about to come between her parents and their dream holiday again. 'I'll come to some sort of understanding with Alex. I'm sure he'll realise there's no need to come here personally every night. I'll ring him.' Yes, she thought with satisfaction. A telephone call would do very nicely. 'Better still, I'll ring you, Anna.'

'I think you're underestimating your sister's powers of persuasion,' said Adam. 'I should think by this point Alex is convinced he personally threw you down the bloody hole. Anna did rather lay it on thick. Anyhow, what's the problem with Alex dropping in here for a few minutes each night?'

'He thinks Hope's a bimbo. I think you should—'

'Hold it there,' Adam replied noting with alarm the determined expression on his wife's face. 'I've told you before, Anna, it's not a good idea to get involved with your sisters' love lives.'

'But Alex is your friend...'

'I'd like it to stay that way.'

'Will you two stop discussing me as though I'm not here? I'm quite capable of sorting out my own problems.'

'Exactly,' said Adam. His wife looked less than convinced, but to Hope's relief she didn't contradict him. She'd just have to rely on Adam's influence on Anna.

A week later, as she sat staring nervously at the clock on the mantel, Hope didn't feel quite as capable of coping with the bizarre situation she'd been forced into. But she had the speech worked out. She'd be polite, but firm.

There's absolutely no need for you to come here again, Alex. Yes, that hit just the right note—confident but not aggressive.

It was eight-thirty, and it was snowing. Fred Wilson, their nearest neighbour, who was looking after the farm while her parents were away, had kindly stacked a fresh pile of logs in the hearth of the inglenook. There was a glass of red wine at her elbow, the smell of the casserole her mother had left was permeating the house and she had a good book. She *ought* to be feeling relaxed. Instead she was jumping at every creak and groan.

She'd knocked thirty seconds off her time getting to the door. She had to dispel any illusion of helplessness that might be lingering in Alex's mind, and these little details were all-important.

I don't know what I'm worrying about; he'll probably be relieved that I don't need him. Not need him? She gave a deep sigh. *If only that were true. Come clean,*

Hope, she told herself, you're really afraid that the moment you see him all those admirable principles of yours will go sailing out of the window. If he tries to make love to you again you might just take what he's offering, even though it isn't nearly enough.

I'm pathetic and feeble, she thought, frowning with self-disgust. What if he thinks I engineered this, put Anna up to it?

This novel idea made her sit bolt-upright. The dimly lit room suddenly took on an entirely different aspect. Seen through his eyes the log fire, subdued light and soft music might take on an entirely more sinister slant. What if, horror of horrors, he thought this was all part of the seduction process?

She pulled herself hurriedly to her feet and hitched her crutches under her arms. The music could go for a start, and she needed light—lots more light!

Her shriek would have done justice to a banshee.

Of course she shrieked. Anyone would if they came into contact with a solid chest of large proportions in a house that ought to contain nobody but herself.

'For crying out loud, woman, you nearly gave me heart failure!' Alex took her by the shoulders and regarded her as if she was mad.

'*You!*' she spluttered indignantly. 'What about me? What do you think you're doing, skulking about? How exactly did you get in?' Her indignation at having her set piece ruined was growing by the second.

'Get in? A key, of course. The one your mother gave me. My God, you're still shaking. Anna said you were nervous about being alone out here, but I thought she was exaggerating.'

'She didn't tell me she'd given you a key,' said Hope, nursing a strong sense of injustice. With a family like

mine, who needs enemies? she reflected bitterly. 'And
I'm not nervous! You startled me, that's all.'

'I had no idea you were so highly strung.' She could
detect a hint of criticism in his tone.

'I'm not a horse, and neither am I of a nervous disposition. I wasn't expecting to walk into...' Her eyes
rested momentarily on the breadth of his shoulders, clad
in the ankle-length waxed coat he wore. 'An obelisk in
my sitting room. You might have knocked.'

'I did, several times, but you must have been en-
tranced by the music.' The lines around his eyes deepened as a scornful expression flickered into his eyes. 'Do
you *like* that sort of thing?' he asked as the soulful ballad
continued to unfold to his unappreciative ears.

Just as well I wasn't setting a seduction scene, Hope
thought with an ironic smile. 'Actually, yes. What's your
style, Alex? Don't tell me you're an ageing head-
banger?' she mocked gently.

'I'm more classically inclined myself, and if I'm feeling romantic a nice slice of Puccini usually fits the bill.
But in the context of our relationship I don't suppose
that's relevant.'

It wasn't easy to break the hold of those challenging
grey eyes. There was something menacingly attractive
about his stare. 'Very true, but it does surprise me you
ever feel *romantically* inclined. You reduce everything
down to its lowest common denominator.' Was that honesty or just a fear of deeper involvement? The puzzle
brought a small furrow to her smooth brow.

'And that offends you?'

'It's irrelevant to me,' she said grandly. 'And if you
don't mind I'm quite capable of standing without assis-
tance.' She looked pointedly at his big hands. The usual
thing happened and a wave of aching helplessness
washed over her. She was ready for it and she hardly

even swayed. 'By the way, you're steaming,' she observed prosaically. She'd die of humiliation if he guessed how she was feeling.

'So I am.' He let her go and began to shrug off the big coat from which the moisture was visibly evaporating before the roaring fire. He shook his head and a myriad of tiny droplets spun from his hair. Some landed on Hope's skin—tiny, icy specks of moisture. 'It's snowing heavily.'

'Then it was stupid of you to come here,' Hope pointed out. The farm was quite high up, and the weather was always worse here than down in the town.

'I said I'd come, so I have,' he said, with a note of finality that she found extremely frustrating.

'Even though it's totally unnecessary?'

He flicked her an assessing look. 'I'll hang this in the hall to dry, shall I?'

'Why ask me?' she called after him. 'You seem to be quite at home.'

He returned moments later. 'Don't look for hidden agendas, Hope,' he said bluntly. 'You made your position quite clear and I don't have the inclination or energy for coercion. So you can stop looking at me as if I'm about to leap on you,' he said drily.

'That's a relief,' she responded flippantly, to cover the disturbingly ambiguous feelings this statement inspired. So she only had her own base urges to worry about now. The thought gave her scant comfort.

'You do look tired.' The lines of exhaustion that bracketed his mouth worried her. There was a grey tinge to his skin too, and the dark smudges beneath his eyes suggested that he hadn't had enough sleep. 'Sit down.' Why did I say that? she wondered in an agony of self-recrimination. You should be showing him the door, not creating an atmosphere of welcome.

Alex looked as if he wondered why too, but rather to his own surprise he followed her suggestion. 'I had a meeting in Birmingham this morning and I had to make a detour on the way back. As usual, at the first sign of a snowflake the whole road system is grinding to a halt. It was one of those days when you have to drive defensively. That weird section of society who feel they're immortal were out in force. Suicidal tendencies don't begin to cover it. I also had to change a tyre on the hard shoulder, which was the finishing touch to a very frustrating day.' He moved his hand and it nudged her wine glass. Quick reactions stopped the contents from spilling.

He might be tired, she reflected, but he isn't slow. I'm sure the last thing he wanted to do was come here. It was terrible to be designated a boring chore. I expect he's longing for his own hearth. He obviously works too hard, she decided with a frown.

'This is your seat.' He made as if to move.

'No, it's all right. I'll sit here.' The back of her knee made contact with the sofa. 'Do you want some wine?' The offer came out in a rush. Silently she despaired of her behaviour. A little chink of vulnerability in his armour and she was getting all mushy and protective. Alex is the last person in the world who needs protecting, she reminded herself sternly.

His slanted brows shot towards his hairline. 'To celebrate our truce? I'm all for that.'

'Don't push it, Matheson,' she growled, without any real conviction. When his eyes smiled he really was incredibly attractive. He was just incredibly attractive full stop.

'Let me get the glass,' he said as she reached into the bureau cupboard.

'Don't you dare. I'm getting tired of telling people I'm not helpless.'

'No, but you are vulnerable. Thanks,' he said as she handed him the wine glass. 'How many times were your parents cut off last winter?'

'I don't know; I wasn't here.'

'But you'll agree they were?'

Hope nodded reluctantly. 'We usually are.'

'Then I can perfectly understand your mother's concern; it's about time you did too. I'm all for independence, but I've no great admiration for stupidity!'

'Are you calling me stupid?'

'Let's not start name-calling.' He looked at her over the top of his glass and Hope viewed his pacifism with suspicion. 'Shall we just take it as read that you're as obstinate as a mule?' he continued smoothly, ignoring her snort of outrage. 'I'm the closest neighbour you've got if anything goes wrong, and it's very little inconvenience for me to spend ten minutes every day to check things.' He made it sound as though she was making a fuss about nothing.

'The Wilsons are closer,' she pointed out pedantically.

'As the crow flies,' he agreed, 'but they'd have to trek across four fields to get here if the roads were blocked. They are already looking after the livestock, aren't they? Do you want to impose on them even further?'

'I still think it's totally unnecessary.' She already knew she'd lost. It was awful! She was going to see him every day for the next three weeks. Every day she'd be the chore he had to do at the end of the day. Every day she'd be in a state of breathless anticipation by the time he arrived. All that emotional turmoil, and for what? I can't cope with all this anticlimax, she thought bleakly.

'Fortunately,' he said wearily, closing his eyes, 'I'm not too bothered about what you think.' His big body slumped in the armchair.

She'd had a puppy once that could do that—fall asleep

without warning—often in the strangest locations. This was the first time she'd seen a person do it.

'Don't fall asleep!' Panic sharpened her voice.

'What…? God, no.' He rubbed his hands over his face roughly and shook his head 'Sorry. It must be the heat.'

'It doesn't matter,' she responded gruffly. She couldn't help feeling fascinated by the youthful cast to his features as he'd hovered on the brink of sleep. All the usual hard wariness had momentarily vanished. Don't go confusing him with your puppy, Hope, girl, she told herself firmly. 'I'm sure you've got things to do.' Things involving slender female bankers probably, she thought darkly.

'Sleep.' He had the stamina and the discipline to get by with very little of this commodity, but just lately he'd been pushing it.

'You should eat,' she told him sternly. 'I was just about to—' She stopped herself in the nick of time. Hope wasn't used to being distant and unfriendly. The warmth of her natural personality kept peeking out at all the wrong moments.

Alex was watching her, a trace of amusement in his eyes. 'What were you about to do?'

'Eat.' She gave a sigh of defeat. 'You can have some if you like. There's plenty.' That was an understatement. Her mother hadn't adjusted her quantities when she'd filled the freezer with ready-to-heat meals. 'The dogs will have it if you don't.'

Obviously she categorised him in the same file as canines; that did wonders for his ego. 'Your hospitality has a warmth and charm all of its own,' he responded gravely. 'I'd be delighted to dine with you.'

'Don't expect it every night.'

'I'll try and keep my appetite in check.'

'Humph,' she snorted, turning her face way so he

couldn't see her blushing like a teenager at the sly *double entendre*.

'This is delicious.'

Hope nodded, pleased he appreciated her mother's cooking. She laid her fork to one side and watched with fascination as he made substantial inroads into the food.

He looked up and intercepted her stare. 'The stuff they fed me at lunchtime was pretty, but not very substantial.'

'And there's a lot of you to fill.'

'Exactly.'

'Do you cook?'

'When I've someone to cook for. It's too much bother just for one.'

Hope nodded agreement, and wondered how often he had someone to cook for. 'Have you always lived at the Mill?' Considering the Mill House was barely a mile from the farm, it was strange she'd never been inside.

Alex pushed his plate to one side and leaned back in his chair. 'Dad bought it at the same time he did the old warehouse. He never got around to converting it until the board booted him out as chairman.' Despite the bland delivery Hope saw the tell-tale tightening of the small muscles around his mouth. 'Before then we lived over the job, so to speak. There's a flat at the factory. Dad and Eva had a place in town, of course, but that was a child-free zone.'

'Why did they do that? Boot him out?'

'You're very curious tonight.' The expression in his eyes was close to hostility, and she was surprised when he saw fit to reply. 'Matheson's is and always has been a profitable venture from the outset. The banks loved it—it was an investment that paid off. The only fly in the ointment was Dad—he just didn't fit into their world. He didn't have the right school tie; he wasn't one of them. His style could be aggressive and he trod on a lot of people's toes—they didn't forget.

'When a freak set of circumstances gave them the chance to cast doubt on his ability to run the company they milked it for all it was worth. Conspiracy is a hard word, but I think on this occasion it's justified. The last thing he expected was to be stabbed in the back,' he reflected grimly. 'That's what made it worse somehow.'

'But you're the boss now?'

The expression on his hard features had a savage element that made her shudder involuntarily. 'I decided I was going to reclaim the firm the day my father came back home a broken, disillusioned man. I did it, and possibly there's some flaw in my character but I enjoyed it—I enjoyed making the people who had destroyed him taste their own medicine.'

The ruthlessness in him had never been more apparent than at that moment. He would make a truly devastating enemy. This neither repelled nor attracted Hope; it was just part of what he was.

'I didn't mean to be nosy,' she said softly. 'It's just considering you're, in your own words, our closest neighbour, I don't know much about you. You're not really the sort of neighbour who drops in for tea, biscuits and a cosy gossip.'

'Dad was never really accepted as part of the community. I don't suppose it occurred to me to do it.'

'Are you trying to tell me your father was some sort of social outcast?' she said sceptically.

'He may have made a fortune, but to some people he never stopped being the ex-miner with the funny accent.'

'That's ridiculous, Alex. People aren't like that,' she protested.

'You're wrong, Hope, that's *exactly* what people are like,' he said harshly.

'It seems to me,' she retorted, 'that it's you who has the problem. My mum and dad have never judged anyone on their background in their lives,' she responded indignantly.

The shake of Alex's head conceded this. 'It was partly the old man's fault. He did have social aspirations of the most transparent kind, and marrying Eva gave him a pathetic sort of desperation to please her. It was the sort of people he desperately wanted to be accepted by who never really did so. In business his talent won him respect, but I think he tried too hard to fit in socially. The right clothes, the right car, the right school for his son and even eventually the right wife.'

'And that embarrassed you?'

The glance that Alex shot her was tinged with shock. 'If I'm honest, I think it did,' he admitted ruefully. At a very early age he'd vowed never to be called a social climber. People would have to accept him on his own terms or not at all.

'And that's why you never make the first move. If anyone wants to be your friend *they* have to make the effort. Don't you think you're a bit big to be afraid of rejection?'

She held her breath. She was taking a bit of a risk. These revelations had given her insight into Alex Matheson's character. His aloofness was suddenly a lot easier to understand. She relaxed as the flare of anger in his eyes was swiftly replaced by a grudging amusement.

'You play dirty, Hope.'

'It depends on the company I keep.' This unfortunate comment reminded her of the sort of company Alex imagined she kept, and the humour faded from her face. 'There's no pudding,' she said abruptly. It wasn't going to do her any good to build up some cosy rapport. The fact Alex despised her was going to get in the way whichever way you looked at it.

'Watching your weight?' His eyes dropped to skim over the lush curves of her figure.

'An occupational hazard—along with the drugs, debauchery and general dissipation.'

'Are you trying to tell me that's not the case?' The way his lip curled scornfully made her blood boil. It was so unfair. *Life's* unfair. Cut out the self-pity, Hope!

'Are you trying to tell me there's not a lot of corruption and underhand dirty dealing in the wonderful world of big business?'

'Are you questioning my integrity?' he asked stiffly.

He really couldn't see the double standard; it was amazing. 'I wouldn't do that, Alex, unless I was very sure of my facts,' Hope shot back swiftly.

There was a startled pause. 'That's a very neat way of calling someone a narrow-minded bigot,' he breathed admiringly.

If the cap fits, Mr Matheson, dear. 'I'm working under the constraints imposed by your being my guest. Mum was always a very liberal parent, but she has some very strict rules about things like that.'

'And have you always kept your mum's rules in mind, Hope?'

'Once I got past the rebellious stage.'

'I had a rebellious stage, too,' he admitted, rather surprisingly.

'You can remember that far back?' she gasped admiringly. A deeply wicked grin revealed the dimple in her left cheek. 'Did it involve motorbikes—the large, noisy variety?'

'Amongst other things.' His nostrils flared. Did she know that the husky intonation in her voice was sheer torture?

Hope gave a soulful sigh. 'It was an unfulfilled ambition of mine during my dissident period. Young men with motorbikes were strictly forbidden, you see,' she explained. 'I think it was more the motorbikes than the young men that worried Mum. She didn't want any of her daughters ending up in plaster.' She regarded her plastered leg with a quizzical smile. 'Not infallible, my mum.'

'And are you still attracted by forbidden fruit?' Alex's brooding regard had darkened with desire as he watched her animated face, the graceful gestures of her elegant hands. She was incredibly beautiful, but it wasn't just that—it was the aura of warmth she emanated. Mysterious feminine allure and child-like honesty was a bewitching combination. A combination that was eating away at his better judgement.

It had been stimulating, verbally sparring with him, and *wallop!* He'd had to go and spoil it. 'Why not just get straight to the point, Alex? Don't start being squeamish now, ask me outright if I often sleep with married men!'

'Actually, I was thinking of offering to dig my old leathers out of mothballs.'

The breath escaped from her lungs in a soundless gasp. The message in his eyes would have been impossible to misinterpret. 'That wouldn't be necessary,' she said huskily. 'I've never met anyone as attractive as you.' That's it, Hope, she congratulated herself. Play hard to get, why don't you?

'They probably wouldn't fit anyway. I've developed a bit since those days.'

'I can imagine,' she croaked hoarsely. She *had* imagined, in some detail. The heat crawled over her skin as her rampant imagination did its worst.

'I'm older than you.'

'I'm prettier than you.'

'Granted…' The humour that twitched his lips didn't reach his eyes. They were intent, purposeful and dark. They said things that made dark wings flutter deep in her belly.

'We could keep this up all night.'

This time the humour did reach his eyes. 'That could be a mite optimistic.'

She flushed at this crude witticism. 'About Lloyd…' Now was probably the time to explain about the Lloyd situation, before things got out of hand.

'We've all done things we regret, Hope.'

'You don't understand, Alex…' she said urgently.

He moved from his side of the table and came towards her. 'I understand,' he growled. 'I understand I want you so badly I can't think straight.' He drew her to her feet, or rather foot, and his hands about her waist pulled her hard against him.

Hope leaned heavily against him, allowing his body to support her weight. There was no question that he didn't have the strength. His fingers pushed into the thick luxuriant mesh of her hair and her eyes closed as he lifted it, letting the silky tresses fall through his fingers.

A small contented sound escaped her lips. This was where she wanted to be—it felt so *right*. The heat of his body penetrated through the thin wool of the turtleneck she wore. Her sensitised breasts rubbed against the iron hardness of his chest. She luxuriated in the glorious sensation. The contrast between his angular solidity and her own softness continued to excite her.

'A glowing angel,' he murmured throatily against her ear. The waft of his breath on her skin sent shivers of sensation vibrating through her body. His mouth hungrily nuzzled her lower lip, tantalising. He caught the pink tender flesh between his teeth and tugged gently.

When his tongue began to trace the outline of her lips she moaned.

'Do you want to taste me as much I want to taste you, Hope? You can feel how much I want you, can't you?' The instinctive sinuous thrust of her hips caught against the hardness of his arousal, and she felt the shock of contact vibrate through his magnificent body.

'It hurts,' she whispered. He pulled away far enough for his eyes to focus on hers. 'Wanting you this much hurts, Alex!'

There was nothing covert about the savage satisfaction that expanded to fill his eyes. 'I know.'

Her heart pounded slowly in dizzy expectation. 'About Lloyd…' She didn't want anything to get in the way. This was going to be perfect.

He swore. 'For God's sake!'

'But you don't understand. It isn't the way you think,' she said with compelling urgency. She ran a shaky hand over the hard contours of his face. His skin was faintly damp. 'It isn't something I'm ashamed of…'

'I don't want to hear this.'

'You have to, Alex.'

'Maybe you get turned on, reliving the lurid details of your antics with previous lovers, but I don't.'

Hope recoiled from the contempt in his eyes. I'm a fool, she realised with black despair. This isn't any different than the last time—he still despises me.

'What are you doing?' Being picked up as though she was a small delicate thing was a unique sensation.

'Where's your room?'

'Put me down, Alex. I don't think Mum intended you to be quite so literal about tucking me in at night.' Her attempt at lightening humour fell on deaf ears. He was kicking open doors with his booted foot as he strode along the hallway. The study, which had been temporarily converted as her bedroom, was one of the last he approached.

He backed in through the door to protect her injured leg. The hanging rail crammed with her clothes and the vivid Provençal pattern on her quilt cover were incongruous flashes of colour against the book-lined walls. The scent of her perfume hadn't quite overpowered the years' accumulation of pipe tobacco, but it overwhelmed Alex—*she* overwhelmed him. Where Hope Lacey was concerned he had tunnel vision. He couldn't think about anything else but possessing her.

He tugged back the quilt and laid her down. Hope didn't even notice the fact that her skirt was bunched around her middle, revealing the lacy edges of her loose silky pants. His eyes never left her face, and the stark expression of raw desire there appalled and excited her. He pulled off his jacket, tugged his loosened tie over his head and began to flick open the buttons on his shirt.

Each frantic, jerky movement ate deeper into her control. His white shirt hung open and she could see the strongly defined musculature of his torso. He was strength and power, without an ounce of surplus flesh to spoil the sculpted effect. This didn't surprise her; Alex was a disciplined man, who didn't surrender to self-indulgence.

'Surrender'—the word evoked a ravishing image of his body astride her own. She couldn't take her eyes off him. The breadth of his shoulders and chest narrowed dramatically as it merged with his flat washboard belly, and the dark hair that generously covered his chest narrowed to a thin line that disappeared under the waistband of his trousers. His hands moved to the belt that circled his waist.

'You can't!'

'You have to be joking!' The muscles in his throat

worked convulsively as he paused. 'Are you trying to tell me this isn't what you want?' When she didn't reply his face hardened into lines of hard determination and a spasm of annoyance contorted his features. 'I don't care about your past, your lovers—there, does that satisfy you?'

Not when he said it like that, she thought, torn between her own deep, driving need and her conviction this was the wrong way to start a relationship—any relationship—with so much misunderstanding between them.

'This is a unique moment that is never going to come back, Hope. It's up to us both to make of it what we choose. If you send me away you'll always wonder.' His deep voice was silkily insidious. 'Forget about the past,' he advised, 'and the future. We have here and now.'

Hope was well aware of the flaws in this argument. Consequences of the present had a habit of haunting the future. Maybe this *was* going to be the only time for them, a persuasive voice persisted. But wasn't wondering the safer option?

CHAPTER FIVE

'YOU were very sure I'd say yes, weren't you?' Hope lifted her head from its cradle on his chest and looked enquiringly into his face.

'If you hadn't, anaesthetic is the only thing that would have got me through this night sane—with the possible exception of a bottle of malt.'

His sincerity brought a satisfied smile to Hope's lips. Did Alex always look this relaxed and mellow afterwards? she wondered. Her secret blush was hidden by the darkness. She had no regrets. Only a crazy person could have regretted anything so mind-blowingly perfect.

'Will you class me as an insensitive brute if I fall asleep?' He pushed aside her hair and pressed his lips to the side of her neck.

'I think you've earned it,' she teased softly.

He slept almost immediately, his head resting on the upper slopes of her breasts. Listening to the regular sound of his breathing, Hope stroked her long fingers through his hair.

She was relaxed, but wide awake. Excited, but calm. Her look of submission hadn't been enough for him. He'd wanted—or maybe needed—to hear her say it. The memory brought a rush of heat to her skin.

'I want you to make love to me, Alex.' The hot, hazy blankness that had entered his eyes had been frightening.

For a split second fear of the unknown had swamped her desire. She'd had little experience to draw on for comparisons, but her brief affair with Hugh had never

78

been frightening or unpredictable. He'd been a generous lover and, even if the earth hadn't moved, she'd enjoyed the warmth and laughter of their intimacy. The raw savagery on Alex's drawn features represented something alien to her. She'd watched the muscles bunch and strain in his arms. He was incredibly strong. What if he lost control…?

'Relax.' He must have caught her sudden flurry of doubt. 'When I said I wasn't going to leap on you I meant it.' He cupped her chin in one hand and she moved her head and pressed her lips to his palm. 'Shall we level things out a bit?' he suggested throatily.

She obediently lifted her arms as he took hold of her sweater and he pulled it over her head. The hardened tips of her breasts peaked further and swelled beneath the white cropped cotton top she wore. It left her curves hidden, but sexily explicit. She knew her body was better than adequate, but despite this confidence, she experienced a sudden anxiety to please.

'I would have worn something a little more adventurous if I'd known.' The sweep of his straight dark lashes hid his expression from her eyes. What was he thinking? Did he like what he saw?

'You can't enhance what is perfect.' He raised his eyes and she knew it wasn't disappointment she read on his face. His features were taut with need, his eyes lightened by silver streaks of raw desire.

She inhaled sharply as his hand came up to cover her left breast. She watched as the flat of his big hand moved slowly over the firm swell. She closed her eyes as her nipple tingled and burned. His hand moved with agonising slowness over the tight, firm flesh of her midriff, stopping only when his fingers slid beneath the waistband of her wraparound skirt.

'How does this thing come off?' His voice sounded thick and hardly recognisable.

The desire that filled her was viscous and honey-sweet. Her tongue felt too slow to form a reply. 'A button, here.' She touched his hand. The contact sizzled through her. 'And here,' she whispered huskily.

'Do it for me.'

The simple request sent an erotic thrill through her body. She raised herself from the pillows and flicked each button open. The skirt unwound and she pulled it free.

Alex took it from her grasp and flung the garment across the room. The muscles in his chest rippled. With a small cry she leant forward and placed both her hands flat against his skin.

'You wouldn't believe how badly I've wanted to touch you.' His muscles contracted under her touch and she felt dizzy with desire. 'How badly I've wanted to taste you.' Her head dipped forward and her tongue lashed experimentally across one hard, flat nipple. Both her arms slid under his arms and her hands curved over his shoulderblades, kneading his hard flesh as she brought her face closer. There was the sound of Alex's harsh breathing intermingled with tiny whimpering noises which Hope didn't connect with herself.

After a few moments Alex's fingers wound into the glistening strands of her tangled hair, and with one hoarse cry he yanked her head away.

Hope's glance was hot and hazy. 'Why did you do that?' she protested. She cast a swift, frustrated glance at the cast on her leg and silently cursed the immobility that took the initiative from her.

'You're driving me crazy!'

'Isn't that the idea?' She wanted to drive him crazy. She wanted to hear him cry out in pleasure.

The darting, sultry glance of her eyes had a way of stripping the civilised veneer that was all he had left to hold his responses in check. 'Definitely,' he agreed firmly. 'Only I'm going to be crippled for life if I don't take these off.' His hands moved to the waistband of his trousers.

He had his back to her as the trousers obeyed gravity. He stepped out of them, and a pair of boxers followed suit. His behind was tight and muscular, and she was still admiring it when he turned around.

'Would *wow* come over as tackily coarse?' She swallowed and felt the colour burn her cheeks. Her flippancy didn't hide the flattering awe in her eyes, and the way his unrestricted arousal stirred seemed to indicate she hadn't overstepped the bounds of decency in his eyes.

He had a body straight out of a fantasy. She swallowed hard as he knelt on the bed. 'Beauty' was a word, but Alex was more than that—*much* more. He was the essence of all things male. And he's mine, she thought gloatingly.

Arms crossed, she pulled her bra top over her head. Free from their Lycra imprisonment, her breasts swayed gently. She smiled as his eyes watched the undulations. Her heart was pounding wildly as she took hold of his wrists and led his hands to the twin warm mounds of flesh.

Alex's expression was almost blank as he looked from her face back to his wrists, imprisoned by an elegant pair of hands. She could almost hear the sound of something in him snapping—although exploding would have been closer to the mark.

His fists opened and his hands accepted the gift she offered. A strange cry ripped from his throat as his mouth came down on hers, driving her back against the mattress. His mouth wasn't gentle; it was hot and hungry. His tongue plunged repeatedly into the warm moistness of her mouth in a deliberate parody of a more intimate invasion of her body. And all the while his mouth plundered hers his hands were moving over her body with feverish haste, moulding her flesh to his needs.

When his mouth moved to her taut, aching breasts, tasting, suckling, her back arched and she cried out without being sure what it was she so desperately needed. She couldn't see any way it would be possible to assuage the hunger he had awoken.

He was astride her, his knees braced either side of her hips. He was too far away, she thought fretfully—too far.

He leant back and deliberately placed the heel of one hand against the soft mound at the apex of her legs. Her head thrashed wildly against the pillow and her body pushed rhythmically against his hand. His fingers slowly curled until he could feel the moist heat through the fine fabric of her pants.

'How do you get these off over the plaster?' he asked thickly. Before she could reply she heard the sound of tearing fabric. 'I applied a bit of lateral thinking.'

Hope had never heard brute force and impatience called this before, but she didn't pursue the issue—especially as he had begun to stroke the satiny inner aspect of her thighs.

'Alex...' she moaned.

'What, love?' The fine tremors that intermittently racked his powerful frame communicated themselves to her through his fingertips. The skin was drawn tightly over his flushed face; his eyes appeared almost black. He looked as if he was struggling against restraints of his own making.

When his fingers explored deeper, moving delicately into the warm, wet valley between her legs, she opened her mouth to cry out, but the sound of her voice was lost in the recesses of his warm mouth.

'Don't fight it, angel.' The erotic throb of his voice was against the base of her throat. The new growth on his jaw abraded her soft skin. 'You like this, don't you?'

'It's good,' she gasped. 'I don't think I can bear it, Alex!' It was delicate, relentless torture. All there was in her world were the sensations that were building inside her trembling body. Even if she hadn't been tied down by the cast she wouldn't have been able to move; her lower body was paralysed by warm, liquid heat.

'Hold on.' She realised he meant it literally as he placed her hands against the bars of the iron bedstead. 'I like watching you,' he confided huskily, his eyes fixed in fascination on her flushed face, her parted lips and half-closed eyes. 'You can't hide anything from me.'

Her body continued to move restlessly under the delicate expertise of his hands. 'Do you want me to?'

'No.'

It sounded to Hope as if his breathing had gone just as haywire as her own. His big body slid down beside her, and the provocative thrust of his rigid arousal against her thigh made her bite her lips and moan his name softly as a sensual thrill lanced through her.

He was sliding lower, his tongue gliding slowly over her warm, smooth skin, drawing a line down her abdomen. The small indentation above her navel seemed to fascinate him. Hope's hands tightened on the bedhead as he paused to explore with wet, darting forays. One hand moved to one smooth hip, and she felt impelled to apologise huskily.

'I'm sorry—the cast. I'm a bit like a stranded whale.'

He lifted his head and looked consideringly at her supine form. With shocking deliberation he moved both hands between her legs, until the tips of his fingers touched the soft protective thatch. She gave a sigh of relief when he parted her legs. She couldn't swallow; her throat was too dry.

'No, there's no resemblance at all,' he contradicted. 'Ingenuity is one of my strong points. I won't let this—' he touched the cast '—spoil things for you.'

'I was thinking about you.' She applied her tongue to her dry lips.

'Angel, nothing short of divine intervention would spoil things for me at this point.'

'Alex,' she breathed in shock, 'you can't do that!'

'I can.' He sounded very confident about this.

'You can't *want* to do that!'

'I do.' His firm assertion silenced her feeble protest, and after the initial rejection she began to relax. It was electrifying, and the erotic friction sent her swiftly spiralling out of control. The rhythmic lash of his tongue instilled a primitive urge to fight for possession. She needed him to take her completely. In a husky, faltering voice she told him this—she screamed it as her clawed fingers tangled in his hair.

Alex's taut smile was filled with male triumph. He wanted to extend her need to its ultimate limit, even though doing so was a form of torture. To feel her shudder and frantically writhe with want, and to know it was his name on her lips, was more arousing than anything he'd ever experienced.

He was sure this level of intimacy was new to her. But this wasn't the time to wonder at this unexpected discovery.

Alex knelt between her splayed legs and pulled her across his steel thighs. He distributed her weight more evenly as his hands scooped her buttocks. She didn't need to move her injured leg; it was firmly anchored beside his hip. This display of strength was a lot more than impressive; it was primitively arousing.

Tongue caught between her teeth, Hope looked at the point where his sex nudged the triangle of damp thatch between her legs. Hot need flooded through her, and just as she thought she'd die from sheer want he slid forward and up, sheathing himself inside her.

He'd positioned her so that he could set the pace, but she could and did urge him on with her strong pelvic muscles and hoarse but enthusiastic cries of encouragement. She sensed he was holding himself back, and she had no intention of allowing that. She wasn't fragile; she didn't want tentative.

'Is this what you want?' he growled.

'Yes, oh, yes!' she cried as he buried himself up the hilt. She greedily absorbed him. Her hands fought for purchase against the glistening skin of his back. Her head fell against his shoulder as he continued to thrust into her. Her laboured gasps scalded the skin of his neck as the pressure built.

When it came, the release shook Hope deeply. The wave of delight invaded each separate nerve-ending in her body. Her body arched backwards and, head thrown back, she cried his name. Her cries were almost instantly drowned by Alex's gratified groan, and feeling him pulsing within her brought tears of emotional fulfilment to her eyes.

Once she'd started the tears wouldn't seem to stop. Alex's alarm was only brief, and then he appeared to instinctively recognise them for what they were, and he was content to soothe her body until only the occasional hiccough shook her.

'I'm sorry.' She couldn't put into words how profoundly the experience had touched her.

'I think it was a compliment.' He touched the dampness on her cheek.

'It was.' She placed her cheek against his chest and felt the heavy thud of his heartbeat.

She did eventually sleep, and when she woke up Alex was propped up on one arm, watching her. His expression was enigmatic but promising.

'Hello.'

Alex caught his breath. Where he'd been half anticipating wariness and caution, she was all uncomplicated warmth.

'Hello,' he responded huskily. She stretched lithely, hooking one arm above her head and brushing tangled strands of hair from her sleepy eyes. He's never seen a woman with less artifice—strange, when she made her living from creating an illusion.

'How long have you been watching me?'

'Long enough to know you sleep like a baby.'

'I've got a clear conscience.'

He didn't respond to this light challenge, although he did reflect that conscience depended on personal standards. He couldn't believe she was this uncomplicated. People just *weren't*.

The sheet had slipped to reveal the upper slopes of her magnolia-pale breasts. She had the most perfect skin he'd ever seen. One rosy areola peeked cheekily out above the white cotton. He rubbed his finger along the fascinating area and felt the pinkness ruche under his touch.

'You know all my weak spots. I don't know any of yours,' she complained huskily.

He had one big weak spot, and it stood five-eleven in bare feet. Vulnerability wasn't something that made Alex happy, but sliding his hand beneath the covers to touch Hope did. If a man had to be confronted with dilemmas, he reflected, this wasn't such a bad one.

Alex pressed his lips to the inside of her wrist and moved with devastating effect along the inner aspect of her arm.

'Alex...?'

'Mmm...'

'You get a lot of pleasure from foreplay, don't you?' That much had been deliciously obvious the night before.

He lifted his head. 'I get a lot of pleasure giving you pleasure. Are you trying to tell me you didn't—'

'Hell, no.' She quashed that theory swiftly. 'The thing is, sometimes a person can feel a bit... I'm trying to be delicate, here, but it's not easy. A person can feel a bit *urgent*. Actually, the moment I opened my eyes and saw you I wanted... Are you laughing at me?'

'*Moi?*' he said, all smug innocence. 'Go on,' he urged. 'This is fascinating.'

'You're a rat-faced, smug—' She broke off and gave a sigh of defeat. Alex looked startled as she grabbed his hand. '*This* is how I feel,' she said, leading his hand to the slick heat that indicated the degree of urgency that filled her. A voice somewhere told her she'd become totally wanton and shameless, but she was unrepentant. 'I want you inside me—*now*.' A low moan vibrated in her throat as his fingers curled against her parted sex.

'That can be arranged.'

'You beautiful man, you,' she sighed. 'I love you.'

They were seated at the kitchen table eating scrambled eggs when Adam entered the room. He stood stamping his feet on the flagstone floor.

'It's bloody freezing out there—' He stopped midsentence when he finally noticed that Hope wasn't alone.

After one slack-jawed instant her brother-in-law recovered his poise and continued to peel off his gloves. 'Is that coffee I smell?'

'Help yourself,' Hope said, steeling herself for the comments she knew would follow. Alex hadn't betrayed so much as a flicker of discomfiture. She watched enviously as he shovelled another forkful of egg into his mouth. There's absolutely no reason to feel self-conscious, she told herself. But the awkwardness persisted.

'Car broke down, did it?' her brother-in-law asked, leaning against the work surface with a cup of steaming coffee in his hand.

'No. Do you have a problem with that?' Alex placed his elbows on the table and looked squarely at his friend. There was more curiosity than hostility in his voice.

'Why should he?' Hope interrupted tartly at this juncture.

She wasn't even prepared to field Anna's inevitable questions about Alex's intentions, without having Adam start! How the hell am I supposed to reply, she wondered bleakly, when I don't know myself? In Alex's own words, he was only concerned with the here and now. That didn't sound like the basis of a meaningful relationship.

Both men simultaneously shook their heads at her lack of insight into male protective instincts. She could almost feel the bond developing as they exchanged looks. Men! she thought with disgust.

'The eggs look good,' Adam observed.

'Well, you can't have any,' Hope said with scant regard for hospitality. 'And I know you're working the conversation around to a rash of those awful one-liners of yours, so I'm warning you...'

'I'm gone.' Adam placed the coffee cup on the table.

'I've banned Anna from driving today, Hope, so I'm afraid you'll be on your lonesome.'

'I think I'll cope. You really must have got Anna well and truly under the thumb if she lets you lay down the law.' It didn't sound like the Anna she knew.

'The trick is letting her think it was her idea,' Adam replied with a grin. 'I think you'll need a hand to dig out your four-wheel drive, Alex.'

'I'd appreciate that.'

'If you saw Alex's car then you knew he was here,' Hope realised, detecting a certain inconsistency. 'You were...'

'Winding you up?' her brother-in-law suggested. 'Like a lamb to the slaughter, Hope,' he observed, chuckling as he opened the kitchen door.

'And you knew he already knew,' she accused Alex indignantly. He didn't appear to have any trouble deciphering this tortuous statement.

'The Land Rover is parked about six feet from the door. Adam couldn't have gotten in without falling over it,' he pointed out with imperturbable calm. 'You did say it didn't matter if Adam knew I'd spent the night,' he reminded her.

'It shouldn't,' she muttered, eyeing him resentfully. The insensitivity of the male species in general was staggering, she reflected.

'But it does. Would you have preferred I'd slipped away earlier?' The intensity of his gaze made her uncomfortable.

'No.' Though in some ways it would have been easier, she acknowledged. On balance it was preferable to face the speculation of her ever-loving family rather than have him slip furtively away as though they'd done something to be ashamed of. 'This all feels a little strange. I'm not used to breakfasting with men.'

The expressive quirk of one darkly defined brow brought a flurry of panic. 'I usually kick them out the night before.' With a laugh she lessened the impact of her thoughtless confession. Ironically he was far more likely to believe the joke than the truth.

'Shall we do this again?'

'Eat breakfast?'

He frowned impatiently at her flippancy.

'What am I supposed to say, Alex?'

'Yes or no.'

'It's that simple?' It probably was for him. There was no conflict for him, no emotional complications. He was just satisfying a basic appetite.

'That's up to us.'

And that told her absolutely nothing, she thought with frustration. Was it an invitation to establish some sort of official relationship, or a warning not to let things get out of hand? Talk about ambiguous! But it was a bit late to start loving defensively—just love, Hope, she told herself recklessly. Love, and live with the consequences.

'Yes.' He hadn't actually appeared to be awaiting her verdict with bated breath, but he did now look moderately satisfied.

'I can't stay tonight. I've got a guest.'

She pushed aside the irrational wave of rejection that swept over her. 'Fine,' she said calmly. Be adult, Hope, keep it low-key.

'I'll call in about nine to check things are all right.'

'You don't have to.'

'Accept help graciously, Hope.'

'That'll be the day,' she responded, with a spark of humour. She was going to have to do something fairly drastic about this obsessional craving she was fast developing for his company.

'I'll chop some more logs before I go. I noticed the

store was getting low. Unless you prefer to wade through a foot of snow to do it yourself?'

'Look,' she said, placing her forefingers at the corners of her mouth and tugging her lips into a grimace. 'I'm smiling graciously.'

He was early. That was the first thought that entered her head when she heard the banging at the back door. Heart pounding, she hurried across the flagstoned floor, cursing her crutches. She fumbled to lift the latch and tried to subdue the breathless smile of welcome that her features insisted on forming.

'Lloyd!' The anticlimax was intense. Foolishly she felt like sitting on the cold floor and sobbing like a baby. 'Whatever are you doing here?'

'I knew you'd be mad with me, but can I come in? I had to leave the car about two miles down the lane. To be truthful, honey, if I'd known that you hailed from the back of beyond, I'd have stayed in my centrally-heated hotel room—guilty conscience or no.' He blew on his bare fingers and his breath billowed white in the icy air.

'You'd better come in.'

'Thank God for that. I thought you were going to kick me out into the snow.'

'The thought has some appeal,' she admitted drily.

'Jeez, your poor leg,' he said as she hobbled across the room. 'You've not been having a good month, have you?'

'Not so as you'd notice.' A smile hovered on her lips—things had been looking up recently.

'What can I say? I owe you big time.'

'Just so long as you know it,' Hope responded tartly. 'Put your coat by the Aga; it's drenched,' she instructed as he shrugged off his padded coat. Even without the coat Lloyd was a big, chunky sort of man. He was handsome in a beaky-nosed, rugged sort of way. 'Didn't you listen to the weather forecast?'

'Sure, but I didn't think you lived at the end of a dirt track. Did you know there are four gates across it?' he asked as he laid his coat across the back of a chair.

'I'd noticed,' she said, her lips quirking in amusement at the indignant tone in his voice. 'I thought you were a rugged mountain man,' she teased.

'That was way back. These days I'm a more your condo and air-conditioned limo type of man. There's no calluses on these hands.' He extended his well-manicured fingers for her to inspect.

An image of hands that did have calluses flickered into her head. 'You're soft,' she teased, forcing herself to concentrate. Thoughts of Alex were disastrously distracting.

'I'm contrite,' he said seriously. He pulled out a chair from the table and straddled it, placing his hands on the ladder back. 'You have to believe I had no idea that the press would crucify you here too. Shirley and I are really grateful that you kept your mouth shut. Politics is a tough game, but her son got the State appointment, thanks to you, and there's no reason we can't come clean now.'

'That's good news.'

'My dear soon-to-be-ex is going to be mad as hell when she realises we took her for a ride.' This thought seemed to afford him some pleasure.

'I take it this isn't an amicable parting of the ways? So long as I'm not the target of her ire this time.' The last time had been particularly unpleasant.

'You're out of it now, Hope. I just hope poor Shirley can take the press coverage we get.' Lloyd caught her look and had the grace to flush. 'It's different for you, Hope, you're tough.'

Gee, thanks, she thought. Did he honestly think the invasive curiosity of the media had no effect on her? she marvelled. Still, the relief that the charade was over was intense. 'I'll drink to the end of the charade.'

'I thought you'd never ask. Don't you move. I'll sniff out the booze. Tell me,' he said casually, 'I don't suppose you've got a number I can contact Sam at. I must have mislaid the one he gave me.'

'Mislaid?' She shook her head. 'To think I innocently thought guilt and concern for my welfare were the incentive for this visit.'

Lloyd placed two tumblers he'd retrieved from the draining board on the table. He grinned sheepishly. 'So they were. I even brought you flowers, only I left them in the car. I just thought while I was here...'

'You'd wheedle Sam's whereabouts out of me. The man's on his honeymoon, Lloyd. With my sister. She'd never speak to me again.'

'I've got this great project on the burner—I know he'd kick himself if he missed out.'

'Your altruism is inspiring, but the answer's no.'

'Hope...'

'Wheedling won't work.'

Lloyd sighed. 'It was worth a try.'

Despite this assurance, Lloyd continued to try and worm the information out of her through the evening. Hope wasn't really offended—she had no illusions when it came to Lloyd. She liked him, but when it came to business he wasn't sentimental. 'Single-minded' would be a kind way to put it.

'Just my luck I finally meet a woman who can keep a secret at the wrong moment,' he observed as he prepared to leave.

Hope ignored this sally. 'Have you got that torch?' she fussed as he buttoned up his coat. 'These should fit you,' she added, handing him her father's brown leather gloves. 'But as I've said, you're welcome to stay to supper.' She was glad he'd refused. Alex would be here soon, and this could be a classic case of 'three's a crowd.'

'I'll take a rain check, Hope. Perfect fit,' he agreed, pulling on the gloves. 'There's a full moon and a clear sky out there—I won't need a torch. It's freezing hard, but they're promising a thaw by morning, and if I leave my car out there much longer I'll never budge it.' He placed his hands lightly on her shoulders. 'You'll come to the wedding, won't you?'

'Don't you think you should get divorced first?' she teased lightly.

'Point taken. The thing is, we've been living separate lives for so long I don't really feel married any more. To tell you the truth, I never thought I'd ever feel I wanted to try again. There hadn't been much incentive to split with Dallas before I met Shirley. Now I wish I'd done it years ago.'

'Give my love to Shirley.'

'I will,' Lloyd said huskily. 'I'll never forget what you've done for me, Hope,' he said with an uncharacteristic rush of emotion. He kissed her warmly. 'You're one in a million.'

'Really? I'd have given much shorter odds—a sure thing wouldn't be too wide of the mark.' These words were accompanied by an Arctic blast from the open door, which was warm in comparison to the frigid tone.

'Alex, you're early.'

'Obviously.' The clipped word spoke volumes.

'I don't know what your problem is, friend—'

'I'm not your friend,' Alex responded, stating what was already obvious to Hope. Hostility was oozing out of every pore. She didn't need to be psychic to see what conclusion he'd jumped to, walking in and finding her kissing Lloyd.

'Don't speak to Lloyd like that!' Out of dismay and confusion, Hope was emerging furiously angry. If she'd been wondering if Alex had changed his opinion of her, this little display was a very eloquent answer. *I was a fool to think it would be any other way,* she told herself bitterly. *My God, he* wants *to think I'm some sort of trollop.*

'I'll speak to *Lloyd* how the hell I like!'

'Now just hold on—' Lloyd began angrily.

'Shut up!' they both yelled in unison. Blue eyes clashed with grey as they recognised their shared sentiments.

'Just go, Lloyd,' Hope managed in a much calmer voice.

'I'm not leaving you with *him*,' Lloyd replied firmly, casting Alex a look of mistrust. 'God, Hope, you haven't got yourself mixed up with him, have you?'

Hope wished with all her heart she could deny this. It was easy to see why he was reluctant to leave her, she reflected. Alex did look a thoroughly dangerous proposition. His features were as hard as granite and the coiled tension in his body emphasised the physical threat he could represent.

'Lloyd's not as stupid as he looks, Hope—he doesn't trust you. Hell, it must be tough to have a girlfriend who's likely to jump into bed with the first male to knock on the door,' he observed sympathetically.

'Only if there's nothing better on TV.'

Hope still had hold of a bunch of Lloyd's coat material in her fist, and she had felt him stiffen in outrage at this deliberate provocation. Alex was spoiling for a fight, and she had to protect Lloyd from the consequences of any chivalrous action he might be needled into taking. Lloyd might be a large man, but she had no doubt he wasn't a match for Alex. He was soft, sedentary and nice—attributes that were noticeably absent in Alex.

'Listen, Lloyd,' she said urgently, 'I want you to go, please. Don't worry about him.' She cast Alex a cold look of distaste. 'He's all mouth and muscle—most of it between his ears. The only things we'll be slinging are insults. And as Alex's opinion of anything is irrelevant to me, the only injury I'm going to sustain is an earache.'

'Are you sure?' asked Lloyd doubtfully.

'Is he trying to suggest I'd hit a woman?' At another time in another situation Alex's male outrage might have made her smile. Right now she thought she'd never smile again.

'He won't touch me,' she told Lloyd. 'But you're quite likely to end up with a bloody nose,' she predicted confidently. 'And, no, I'm not suggesting you're scared. But, on a more practical note, do you think a black eye is in keeping with your image? Is it Friday you're on the coast-to-coast chat show?' This little reminder had an immediately sobering effect.

Lloyd looked indecisive. Alex watched his brief wrestle with his conscience with an expression of scorn.

'Well, if you're sure...?'

'Since when did I start needing anyone to fight my battles?' She pressed her lips warmly to his and moved towards the door, but Alex's bulk was effectively blocking it. 'Do you mind?' she said haughtily.

The way he clicked his heels and inclined his head was filled with mockery. 'Aren't you going to ask me to leave?'

And give him the opportunity of refusing? No chance. 'Not before I've told you *exactly* what I think of you, and then it won't be a request.' She saw the momentary

Here's a **HOT** offer for you!

Get set for a sizzling summer read...

with **2 FREE ROMANCE BOOKS**
and a **FREE MYSTERY GIFT!**
NO CATCH! NO OBLIGATION TO BUY!

Simply complete and return this card and you'll get **2 FREE BOOKS** and **A FREE GIFT** – yours to keep!

Visit us online at
www.eHarlequin.com

- The first shipment is yours to keep, **absolutely free!**
- Enjoy the convenience of Harlequin Presents® books delivered right to your door, before they're available in stores!
- Take advantage of special low pricing for **Reader Service Members only!**
- After receiving your free books we hope you'll want to remain a subscriber. But the choice is always yours—to continue or cancel, any time at all! So why not take us up on this fabulous invitation, with no risk of any kind. You'll be glad you did!

306 HDL C26C

106 HDL C252
(H-P-OS-06/00)

▼ DETACH HERE AND MAIL CARD TODAY! ▼

surprise in his eyes. Yes, the offensive was definitely the way to go. If Alex was expecting her to meekly stand there and accept all the vile things he would undoubtedly fling at her, he could forget it!

'The suspense is killing me.'

'Don't raise my hopes,' she hissed. She pinned a smile on her lips as she turned to bid Lloyd farewell.

He'd been listening to their swift interchange with a troubled expression. The undercurrents were enough to make him feel as if he'd outstayed his welcome.

'Safe journey, and as I said, give my love to Shirley.'

'I feel bad leaving you...'

'To say I'm a big girl would be an understatement.'

Lloyd stepped out into the icy farmyard. 'I don't know what your problem is,' he shouted to Alex. 'But this girl is pure gold, and if you can't see that you're blind!'

Hope gave a last wave and closed the door. The expression she glimpsed on Alex's face as she turned gave her the impression he was surprised by the vehemence of Lloyd's parting shot.

'Who's Shirley?'

She hadn't expected that, and for an instant she was thrown into confusion. Since Lloyd had given the all-clear she'd been planning when and how to tell Alex about Shirley. Whilst it might have been nice if he'd not needed explanations, her practical nature had accepted it was unrealistic to expect this.

'Lloyd's mother,' she lied perversely.

It hurt to recall how recently she'd decided that bed would be the best place to tell him the whole story. Tell him how nice and extraordinarily ordinary Shirley was; tell him how it had been a very sensitive time for her son, who had political aspirations, how being associated with a very public divorce might have ruined his chances. Any wild ideas she'd had when he walked in of telling him the truth when he'd calmed down had long gone. She felt too betrayed by his distrust to want to offer explanations any more.

'Don't tell me he's taken you home to the family.'

His scorn banked up her sense of desolation. Nothing she could say or do was going to change his mind. A perverse vindictive streak in her wanted him to dig himself deeper. She wanted to think of him squirming when he learnt the truth, as he inevitably would. If he dared to come crawling back she'd take great delight in laughing at him, she decided confidently.

'I've met them,' she replied truthfully. Lloyd had roped her into persuading his niece to finish her education before she embarked on a modelling career. The whole family had been embarrassingly grateful.

'Did you tell him the bed was still warm from me, or doesn't he care?' In his mind's eye he could see the tumbled bedclothes. 'What sort of warped relationship do you two have?' he asked in disgust. 'It must be a pretty big carrot he's dangling this time if you're willing to…'

'Willing to what, Alex?' she asked, with a coolness that hid her growing anger and disgust. His self-righteous attitude was really getting to her. 'Willing to take him to my bed, not you? Aren't you guilty of making some pretty big assumptions? What makes you think that would be a sacrifice?'

Alex caught his breath sharply. The thought of another man's name on her tongue as her pale body convulsed in the throes of passion made a red mist dance before his eyes. His hands clenched and unclenched as he fought for control. 'If you're trying to tell me I come second best to *him*,' he spat contemptuously, 'don't waste your breath.'

'Oh, Alex,' she taunted gently, 'don't take it so personally. You've probably done me a favour,' she mused thoughtfully. 'I think I was in danger of taking what I had for granted. I was in danger of becoming blasé about cultured, sophisticated men. But I don't really belong here any more.'

'Glad to have been of service.'

The vicious satisfaction she'd felt as she'd seen her words find their mark dissipated. It could be I've gone too far, she reflected, feeling for the table behind her legs. The expression in his eyes made her wish she had the false security of the table between them. She'd primed a bomb and now she didn't know how to defuse it.

'Why make excuses, Hope?' he said in a dangerously quiet tone. 'It's just sex you like. I was wrong to take it personally. It's not just me you can't get enough of. To think I thought I'd been wrong about you.' A spasm of self-contempt contorted his taut features. 'I had my apology all rehearsed.' The nerve beside his mouth jerked erratically.

'How dare you be so sanctimonious?' she cried, sick to the stomach. He'd let *her* down, not the other way around. It was his distrust that had come between them. 'Sex is healthy and natural so long as things are going the way you want. So long as I play by your rules. Aren't you being just a tad perverse, Alex? Wasn't my reputation half of the attraction, if you're honest? Know what I think?' she flung at him. 'I think under all that disgust you're plain and simply jealous as hell!'

He moved towards her and she didn't have the space or mobility to escape. 'Oh, you're right, angel.' He pushed his face up to hers and grinned savagely through clenched teeth. 'I am. But don't get your hopes up. I wouldn't touch you with a barge-pole. Even if my stomach could bear it, women with the morals of an alley cat are a health hazard these days—literally.'

She winced as the door slammed behind him. She felt too drained to cry. Numb and strangely empty. Falling in love wasn't the occasion for joy and celebration she'd always naively expected. Love sucks! she thought, wiping a solitary tear from her face with the sleeve of her sweater.

Anna-Bird exercises. The phone light came on in such rapid . . . .

CHAPTER SIX

HOPE flicked on the angled lamp beside her bed. Three-thirty. She shivered as the cold night air penetrated the thin cotton of her nightshirt. Reluctantly she swung her legs out of bed and her bare foot blindly sought her slipper whilst she lifted her crutches from their resting place beside the bedpost.

The newborn lamb Fred Wilson had pleaded with her to temporarily foster needed feeding. Hope didn't mind—it had always been one of the nicer tasks around the farm.

She cried out in shock as her foot was plunged into icy water. Drawing her foot back to the bed, she peered over the side. 'Oh, God!' Several inches of icy water were swirling sullenly over the floor. 'I don't believe this,' she muttered, her pulses racing in panic.

The impulse to draw the covers over her head and pretend nothing had happened was strong. That didn't work when you tried it earlier, she reminded herself sourly. Telling herself she *wasn't* devastated hadn't prevented her eyes being puffy in the aftermath of last evening's orgy of abject misery—an orgy that had lasted deep into the night!.

Gritting her teeth, she hopped to the opposite side of the room, her plastered leg extended before her. She sat on the edge of her father's desk and picked up the telephone receiver. As much as it galled her, there was no way she could cope with the present emergency with her leg in plaster. Pride would have to take second place to practicality on this occasion.

'Anna, thank goodness.' The phone had been speedily answered. 'Sorry if I woke you. Oh, you were feeding the babies. Of course there's something wrong—I wouldn't be phoning at three in the morning to say hello. Sorry, I'm just a bit overwrought,' she apologised, with admirable understatement. 'The thing is we've got a water leak here. No, I've no idea where it's coming from. I haven't had the guts to venture out of my bed so far. Of course I'm alone!' she added indignantly to her sister's query. So Adam had been talking, had he? she thought grimly as hot colour stained her neck. 'Could I beg a bed—just for the night? If Adam could come over I'd be really grateful.'

She listened in silence as her sister explained that Adam had been called into the hospital to perform some sort of miracle to save a biker's leg.

'I'll send him along just as soon as he gets back,' Anna promised. 'Don't try to do anything,' she warned sternly.

As if I needed reminding I'm helpless, Hope thought, hanging up. She didn't waste her time, though, and by the time she eventually did hear sounds of activity in the hallway she'd swathed her plastered leg in a large plastic bag to protect it from the water, and dug out an old wellington boot from the motley selection that were stored in a cupboard. She'd put on a padded jacket over her nightshirt and shoved some clothes in an overnight bag. She'd belatedly remembered that electricity and water didn't mix, and a torch was now her only illumination

'I know I'm being helpless and hopeless, Adam, but...' She pointed the thin yellow beam at the doorway. The words dried in her throat and her eyes opened wide with horror that was swiftly replaced by anger. 'Get the hell out!'

'All in good time,' Alex replied in a cold, clipped

voice. 'Your sister phoned me and asked me to "ride to the rescue." I think those were her words.' He placed the storm lantern he carried on the bureau. His expression was hidden from her in the shadows.

'I'd prefer to drown.' It couldn't be much worse than the sick churning in her belly, and it might not be such an inaccurate prediction. The water was obviously still rising.

'Don't overplay the drama or I might give you your wish,' he grated. 'Didn't it occur to you to switch off the water?'

'What do you think I am, stupid? The stopcock is in the cellar of the dairy next door, down a flight of stairs. I'm not suicidal.'

'You just prefer drowning to my company!'

Alone again, Hope drummed her fists on the bed in frustration. This couldn't be happening! Anna had probably imagined she was being helpful. Dear God, this had to stop. She couldn't go around beating her breast and tearing her hair—not publicly anyway. Under the circumstances she had little alternative but to cope with being thrown into Alex's company. She tried to view this prospect calmly, with dispassion, and failed miserably.

'Is there much damage?' Dignity and forbearance, Hope, she silently encouraged herself.

'It's a mess,' Alex said abruptly. 'The cold water tank in the attic appears to have burst. There's a river running down the stairs and some plaster down in the hall.' He stepped farther into the room. 'I turned the water off, and the electricity, but there's nothing much else I can do tonight.'

'The responsibility of dealing with my parents' disaster hardly falls to you.' The haughty mask slipped as she thought of what would await her parents on their return.

'What a thing to come back to,' she wailed. 'I've wrecked the house.'

'There's no point blaming yourself.'

Hope's head lifted and she glared at him, her blue eyes swimming with unshed tears. 'I wasn't!' I don't suppose *his* waterpipes would dare burst, she thought resentfully.

'Good. How do you want to do this?'

'Do what?' she asked belligerently.

'How do I carry you out?' he elaborated. 'With dignity and a minimum of fuss, or like a sack of coal, kicking and screaming?'

'Coal neither kicks nor screams, but I'll do both if you so much as lay a finger on me. I didn't want or request a knight in shining armour to rescue me.'

Alex appeared insultingly ummoved by her dire threats. 'You requested Adam, and as I'm his deputy...'

'If Anna knew what a slimeball you are she wouldn't have asked you.'

'In her ignorance,' he replied drily, 'she did just that, and I intend to rescue you whether you like it or not. A dashing Lochinvar I may not be...'

'You can say that again,' she muttered mutinously. 'He was young,' she added with sweet malice.

'But I'm not leaving without you.'

'Call me unnatural—'

'I wouldn't be so presumptuous.'

Hope's lips thinned. 'But I've never had fantasies about being swept up by a knight on a white charger.'

'The Land Rover's green, and much less temperamental than a horse. Stop stalling, Hope, and swallow your pride. You need help and I'm it,' he said with brutal bluntness.

She swallowed. It was humiliating, but he was right.

She picked up her bag and clutched it to her chest. 'Go on, then. Don't make a meal of it.'

'Gracious to the end,' he muttered as he scooped her up.

The embrace of his arms was distressingly impersonal. A wave of loss threatened to overwhelm her when she remembered the last time she'd been picked up by those strong arms. Then don't think about it, dummy, she told herself severely.

The sight of the ruined hallway, covered by several inches of murky water, drove all personal considerations out of her head.

'This is terrible.'

'Nothing that can't be put right,' he asserted confidently as he pushed a floating umbrella out of his path with the toe of his boot.

'Easy for you to say. Stop!' she yelled dramatically.

'What now?' He ground the words out like a man coming to the end of his patience. He grunted and heaved her a little higher. 'Whatever it is, make it quick. You're not exactly a lightweight.'

Hope's bosom swelled with indignation at this slur. 'The kitchen—Daphne's there.'

'Daphne? Who the hell's she?' Alex asked in bewilderment.

'Don't ask silly questions—hurry up!'

When they reached the room Alex placed her on the kitchen table, an island amongst the wreckage.

'The Aga—quick. The warming oven at the bottom.'

Alex sensed the urgency in her apparently bizarre instructions. 'Is this the time to be worrying about baking?' He pulled open the door, which was already ajar. 'It's alive,' he said, shining the light into the dark interior.

'I should hope so,' Hope responded briskly. Despite

the awfulness of the situation her lips twitched as Alex straightened up with the white woolly bundle in his arms. The big man and the tiny lamb made an incongruous pair. 'The formula's in the fridge—you'd better get that too. And there's a spare tin in the larder—third shelf.'

Without a word Alex handed her the bundle. She opened the zip on her holdall and hollowed out a space for the lamb on top of the designer underwear she'd hastily crammed in. When she looked up, Alex was watching her. The shadows moved over his face, revealing for a split second the distraction on his face.

'Aren't you afraid it'll ruin your things?' he said, rubbing his thumb over the label of a silky negligee that had spilled over the edge of the bag.

'Don't be stupid,' she said, with a scornful expression that clearly placed an orphaned lamb well above clothes—even pretty ones. She tucked the bottles of formula into the pockets of her jacket. 'I'm ready.'

'Does that mean we have permission to place our hands on the royal person?' Alex enquired obsequiously.

Hope was immediately conscious of her haughty expression. 'Don't let it go to your head,' she responded in kind.

'This isn't the way to the Old Rectory,' Hope protested when he didn't take the fork in the track that led down to the main road.

Alex didn't remove his eyes from the track ahead. 'No.'

'Is that it? *No?*'

'What else did you have in mind?'

Hope closed her eyes and winced as he smoothly steered with the flow as the Land Rover skidded and slid on the wet ice. 'An explanation,' she said hoarsely, when the vehicle was headed in a more conventional direction.

'Banish all notions or hopes that I'm kidnapping you from your head.'

Hopes! The unmitigated cheek of the man. Twin spots of colour burned on her cheeks. She bent her head and buried her face in the warm bundle on her lap. His words sent a shivery sensation through her body. Being in his power and having no say in the matter was an appalling thought. Wasn't it? 'Is it too much to ask to know where I'm going?' she replied hoarsely. This wasn't the best time to discover a flaw—a gaping, sinful defect—in her nature.

'As my place is the only habitation I know down this track, I'd have thought that was self-evident. The roads are lethal, and I've no intention of driving any farther than necessary tonight. Besides, I don't think it's the time of night to disturb a household with small children. Anna sounded whacked when she spoke to me.'

'Why not call me inconsiderate and selfish and be done with it?'

Alex manoeuvred the Land Rover through the open gate that led to the Mill House. 'Do you have to take everything so personally?' he asked in exasperation.

Yes, where you're concerned, she thought silently. The converted Mill was a stone building three storeys high. Lights from the empty windows spilt out over the terraced gardens that lined the riverbank. When Alex opened the door she could hear the sound of the river in full spate.

'Put your arm around my neck,' he instructed tersely.

As he gathered her to him Hope was aware of the tension in his muscular frame. She flicked him a half-wary glance in the semi-darkness. Mistake, she thought as awareness sizzled along her nerve-endings. His anger had slipped away for the moment, and what it had been masking was suddenly exposed. The silver glitter of his eyes, the heavy-lidded sensuality of his steady gaze stole the strength from her body.

'Don't do that,' she pleaded huskily.

'Do what?'

'You know wha—!' She let out a yelp and just managed to stop the holdall from falling onto the snowy ground. 'Oh, God, look what you made me do! I nearly dropped Daphne. Are you all right, darling?' she crooned anxiously. At least the spell of sexual tension had been broken, though her feelings about this were distressingly ambiguous.

'My back's seen better days.'

'I wasn't talking to you.'

'How cruel of you to dispel the illusion of concern.'

'I suppose you think I'm ungrateful.' She was struck somewhat forcibly that she had been a bit churlish about being rescued. 'You must be pretty annoyed being dragged from a warm bed on a night like this.'

The studded oak door opened as Alex stepped up to it. 'Thank goodness. I've been so worried.' The big door opened directly into a large sitting room. Hope wasn't much interested in its interior decor at that moment.

The nightgown beneath an oversize man's towelling robe was transparent. In the glamour stakes it left her own utilitarian nightshirt standing. Good breasts were clearly outlined beneath a deceptively modest lace yoke, and she was tall—but not too tall. She could have been anywhere between thirty and forty-five. She had the sort of striking features and strong bones that aged well: nice, dark eyes, an aquiline nose, large mouth and short, well-cut dark hair. She didn't give the impression of a woman who habitually worried, but she did give the impression of elegance, intelligence and strength.

It took Hope only seconds to assimilate all these alarming details.

Alex stepped into the warmth. 'Substitute pig-sick for pretty annoyed,' Hope said in a low voice.

Alex's brief glance held a very definite warning.

The wave of intense nausea passed. It had nothing to do with her if Alex Matheson slept with a hundred women, she told herself. But it didn't make any difference. The fierce sense of betrayal was illogical, but she couldn't lose it. The sheer hypocrisy of his behaviour took her breath away and fanned the flames of her wrath. He had the cheek to criticise her relationship with Lloyd when all along he…! The nausea returned with a vengeance when she dwelt on what he'd been doing all along.

'You should have stayed in bed, Rebecca.'

Hope had a vivid mental picture of Alex slipping beneath the covers and pressing his cold body against a warm, soft, yielding feminine one. Masochistically she dwelt on the powerful image.

'Don't be silly, Alex. I've made up a bed for—Hope, is it?' She smiled with what appeared to be genuine warmth in Hope's direction.

The attitude between them spoke of easy intimacy and long familiarity. The look, the casual touch of her hand on his arm. Jealousy located Hope's most vulnerable spots and stabbed repeatedly with a poison-tipped dart. Oh, God, she looks nice, Hope thought dismally. It would have been so much easier if she'd been unfriendly and hostile. Or at least an empty-headed bimbo. A horrifying truth suddenly presented itself to her. *I'm* the empty sexual experience, the light relief, the bimbo, and *she's* the real relationship. After years of refusing to be type-cast Hope had finally succumbed in a big way.

The attraction of the enormous room, with its lofty ceiling and large stone open grate, big enough to hold a

small tree, was lost on her. Hope wanted to be home—
actually, she wanted to be anywhere but here.

Alex's wet boots had left, wet, snowy imprints on one
of the rugs, which had all the faded splendour of an
original Eastern work of art. Hope noticed that
Rebecca's bare feet were silent on the polished wood
boards and that her feet were long and narrow. It was
easier to dwell on inconsequential details.

The sofa he placed her on was generously propor-
tioned, as were most of the pieces of furniture in the
sparingly furnished room. The rough-plastered walls
were colour-washed a warm shade of burnt sienna, and
plants were trained around what must once have been
the original waterwheel, set in an alcove along one wall.

'You both need a warm drink,' Rebecca said, glancing
with some concern from Alex's expressionless features
to Hope's pale, distraught face.

'I could do with something stronger,' Hope said suddenly.

'Will brandy do, or would you prefer—?'

'Brandy's fine,' Hope interrupted abruptly.

The amber liquid burnt as it went down and pooled
in her stomach, leaving a warm glow. A bleat suddenly
reminded her of her charge.

'A lamb! How delightful.'

'An orphan born too early. She's hungry,' Hope said,
digging into her pocket for a bottle. 'Could you warm
this a little, please?'

'Oh, can I feed her?' Rebecca pleaded, with a childish
delight that seemed out of step with her sophisticated
aura

Hope shrugged. 'If you want to. You've got every
thing else, why not her too? she thought dully. She gave
over her charge reluctantly.

'It's called Daphne.' Alex said drily

'Is that a classical allusion?' Rebecca asked, laughing as she held the lamb up to her face.

'No, she looks like a girl I went to school with. People always wanted to cuddle and pet her too.'

'What happened to your Daphne?' Alex asked as Rebecca disappeared from the room.

'She has five children and three ex-husbands. I can't stay here, Alex!' she hissed, glancing furtively over her shoulder at the closed door.

'Why not?'

'Don't be obtuse! Don't you *care* if Rebecca's hurt?' It would be pretty pointless asking if he cared how she felt. The answer to that question was blindingly obvious.

'Why should Rebecca be hurt?' He continued to loosen the laces on his boots.

'Are you trying to tell me she doesn't mind if you sleep with other women? To think you had the gall to read me the riot act over Lloyd when all along you were coming back here to her. Double standards doesn't even *begin* to cover it!'

She might as well have been talking to the three-feet-thick stone wall behind him for all the impact her scornful words made. He kicked off his boots, and the wet socks followed them. One hand went up behind his head and he leant back into the deeply upholstered sofa—a twin to the one she lay on.

'Don't compare my relationship with Rebecca to yours with Elliot.'

Ironically this was a fair comment—but not for the reason he implied. There *was* one big difference: Lloyd wasn't and never had been her lover. Right at this moment it helped her that Alex thought the opposite. She couldn't match his calculating attitude to sex, but he wasn't going to know that if he imagined she was as casual as him. If he knew I'd actually fallen in love...!

She shuddered. The humiliation didn't bear thinking about.

'She knows that you spent last night in my bed, does she?' she challenged.

'She doesn't, and she won't—unless you tell her.' His steady gaze openly challenged her.

'Don't worry,' Hope choked. 'It's not something I'm likely to boast about.'

'I wasn't worried.' He yawned lazily.

'My God, I pity her!' she said unsteadily

'No, you don't,' he contradicted. 'You're as jealous as hell of her. What's wrong, Hope? Don't you like the idea of my hands on her warm skin? My mouth—'

'Shut up, shut up!' she yelled, placing her hands over her ears to shut out the slyly insidious sound of his voice. 'You're disgusting,' she spat.

'But you liked all the disgusting things I did, didn't you, Hope? Your body responds just thinking about them, doesn't it?' His cruel confidence made her grow pale. 'Is that how you aroused yourself with Lloyd? Did you close your eyes and think of me?'

'You're sick!' Had he just predicted her future? she wondered bleakly. Had he spoilt her for any other man? If it had been just sex, she could have lived with it, but it was her love she'd wasted on this man. What a fool I am, she despaired.

Alex rubbed his closed fist across his cheekbone. The gesture made her realise for the first time how tired he looked. 'That possibility had occurred to me,' he agreed cryptically.

'She fell asleep. So sweet. I've given her the cat basket and put it by the radiator.' Rebecca cinched the belt of the robe about her narrow middle and looked at Alex, a question in her eyes. A person would have needed to be deaf and blind not to notice the atmosphere in the room. Alex just smiled sardonically in response.

'What about the cat?' Hope asked. Rebecca's presence rescued her from any further displays of Alex's warped, but uncannily accurate perception.

'It lost the last of its nine lives in the summer,' Rebecca explained. 'I never did know what you saw in the creature, Alex. It was a horrid, bad-tempered beast.'

'Cat lacked polish, but it had a lot of originality.'

'It scratched me.'

'It didn't like being stroked.'

Alex's eyes sought Hope's. His soft words had conjured up an image of his big hands moving down the curve of her arched spine. He couldn't know...it wasn't possible. She felt cold perspiration break out over her body.

'Perhaps we should get some sleep for what's left of the night,' Alex said slowly as Hope licked her lips nervously.

'Good idea,' Rebecca approved.

Hope nodded. She welcomed anything that gave her the opportunity to escape the scrutiny of those eyes.

The staircase was circular, with a wrought-iron balustrade. Even when she closed her eyes she could smell him and feel the warm strength of him as he carried her up.

Just when she needed them the breathing exercises she'd learnt in Yoga deserted her. Instead of having a calming and soothing effect, they alerted her to the fact that breathing wasn't the autonomic response people liked to believe. Her respirations were painfully laboured and erratic. At least suffocating should be diverting.

'If you need anything just yell.'

She nodded faintly and wished he'd put her down.

'Rebecca will see to the lamb.'

'I couldn't possibly impose...' she began stiffly.

'It'll be her pleasure. She'll dine out on the story for weeks whilst she regales her friends with tales of her bucolic adventures. Will you sleep?'

'If I ever make it to my bed.' She turned her head to look pointedly at the neatly turned down twin divan beside the window.

'Sleep well, Hope Lacey.' His throaty voice had a husky edge that felt like a caress to her body. Does he know I'm aching for him? she wondered dreamily. He adjusted the pillow before he relinquished his hold across her shoulders.

Lying supine, with Alex looming over her, she came close to total panic. She couldn't think; she forgot her own name for the space of several breaths. The divan was low and he was kneeling on the floor, his hands flat on either side of her head. She bit her lip to repress a groan when his hand stroked the hair fanned around her face. She *should* reject his touch, but she couldn't, by word or gesture. Her whole body was infused with a warm, weak longing. No matter how wrong it was, something inside her would always respond helplessly to him. This insight frightened her more than anything in her young life.

The sight of his predatory face, all sharp angles and hard planes, etched itself permanently in her mind before he pressed his mouth to hers with slow deliberation. The slick, silky thrust of his tongue into her open mouth made her moan.

'Do you want me now?' The rasp of his erotic words sent shivers down to her toes. His mouth nuzzled against her earlobe.

Want! Want didn't begin to cover the hunger of her starving senses. 'Why are you doing this to me?' she asked in a tortured whisper. 'Do you hate me that much?

Your girlfriend—mistress—whatever, is only feet away, and you're... What sort of man are you, Alex?'

She felt the convulsive tremor that rippled through his big body. He stood up abruptly and stared down into her face.

'If sin had a face...' he said harshly, then he shook his head, as if to dispel the image of her flushed, aroused features. 'Goodnight.'

She might have managed to sleep for an hour at the most. Were they making love? Or was he sleeping in her arms? The torrid images persistently pervaded her mind. She didn't want to hear the sounds of their love-making, but her ears strained anyway, to catch a tell-tale creak or moan.

She didn't have any make-up in her bag to disguise the ravages of the night before, but fortunately she was blessed with the constitution of an ox. Her glow wasn't quite as luminous as usual, but only the harshest of critics would have noticed. She teamed a short black Lycra skirt with a deep blue cashmere tunic. No one looking at her would have guessed she'd just had the most traumatic twenty-four hours in her life.

'I was going to bring you tea,' Rebecca exclaimed as Hope nimbly hopped into the kitchen. 'How on earth did you get down the stairs?' she asked, looking from the crutches under Hope's arms to the plaster cast on her leg.

'I shuffled on my behind,' Hope confessed. She knew Alex was watching her over the rim of his coffee cup and she refused to let him see how much it shook her just to be in the same room as him. 'I've plenty of padding,' she joked with strained humour. She'd have flown if it meant she could avoid being held by Alex, and of course he'd known it

'Anxious to add your neck to the broken leg, are you?'

'Worried about your insurance premiums again, Alex? I'm already suing him—did he tell you about that?'

'I thought that was all settled.'

'Maybe I want my day in court.' She didn't. She didn't want to pursue it at all. But when Alex had pointed out it was 'just business' he hadn't left her much option. Jonathan would probably have a fit when she distributed the money to charity.

'I'd have thought you'd have had enough bad publicity for one year.'

Hope smiled between set teeth. 'I'm not sure my agent makes fine distinctions like that. Overexposure is something he dreams about.'

'You're joking...right?' Rebecca waited with a bewildered expression for her anxious query to be settled.

'Now that's an interesting question, Rebecca. Hope alternates between flinging my money back in my face and trying to screw me for all I've got.'

'I'm feeling vindictive today.' She let her deliberately ambiguous words hang in the air.

Rebecca looked quite relieved when the doorbell rang. 'That'll be my taxi. Goodbye, Hope, so nice to meet you. Thanks, Alex—and I do mean that,' she said with special emphasis as he picked up her cases. She shrugged on an ankle-length trenchcoat trimmed with fake fur over the black tailored trouser suit she wore. This morning the older woman's confidence was very apparent. There was nothing of the sentimental creature who'd begged to feed a baby lamb left today.

'I'll take you to the station.'

'Don't be silly, darling.'

'Wasn't there something you wanted to say to Rebecca?'

Hope blinked and shot Alex a startled glance. She

hadn't expected him to call her bluff. It was ironic. Whereas her veiled threat had been meant to intimidate him, he looked to be the only really relaxed person in the room.

'Thank you, Rebecca, for all your kindness. Could I share your taxi?' she added in a rush. 'My sister lives the other side of the village.' Her brain had been a bit slow working out the three minus one equation, but now it had she was in a state of blind panic.

'Rebecca is in a hurry—she'll miss her train,' Alex interjected smoothly before the other woman could speak. Hope glared at him in resentment as he ushered the older woman out of the room. He put his head back round the door. 'I admire your restraint. And you'd only have embarrassed yourself if you'd told her.'

When he returned she had seated herself at the table and was sipping coffee with a casual nonchalance she wasn't feeling.

'That was quite a display,' he observed. 'Does frustration always make you so tetchy, or is this the real Hope?' Alex crammed some bread in the toaster. 'You should eat.'

'I rarely do what I should.'

'I noticed that.'

'Where does Rebecca work?'

'London. She's a banker.'

She ought to have made the connection before— Anna's lady banker. If Alex made a habit of sleeping with other women that would explain the tension Anna had noticed in her. Though Hope hadn't noticed any signs of stress. 'Is the distance convenient or inconvenient?'

'If you're trying to get a display of guilt or remorse you're wasting your time. You didn't know Rebecca existed the night we spent together...'

'Too right I didn't!'

'Last night you did.' Hope flushed under the intensity of his stare. 'And yet you'd have let me make love to you with her in the same house.'

'In your dreams,' she lied wildly. She couldn't escape the sobering reality of his words.

He caught the toast as it shot out. 'Perhaps we should compare those some time.' He intercepted her blank look. 'Dreams,' he elaborated. 'Marmalade or honey?'

'I'm not hungry.'

'Honey I think,' he responded, as though she'd not spoken. 'As my mother would say, you look peaky.'

'I don't. I look quite good.'

'Granted. It really is effortless for you, isn't it? Women would hate you in their droves if they suspected how little work you put into your appearance.' The warm expression in his eyes as he bent over and placed the plate before her made her stomach muscles quiver violently. 'Eat anyway.'

She bit into the toast. 'I thought your mother was dead, Alex,' she said tentatively, wondering whether his choice of tense had been accidental.

'Dead! Hell, no, when the old man traded her in she moved back home to Yorkshire.' His lips thinned at the memory and his eyes were bleakly resentful.

'But you lived with him.'

'He was the one with the money. She thought it would be better for me.'

'And was it?' Separated from his mother at a tender age—her heart ached with sympathy. It had been a long time since she'd taken her own stable and happy childhood for granted. Now she knew how rare those magical years had been

'Speculation is a pointless exercise. I prefer to reserve my energies for things I can alter.'

Focus was something Alex was generously endowed with, she silently reflected. 'Do you see her much now?'

'Not as often as I'd like. I've asked her to move down here, but she's a very stubborn, proud lady.'

'She must have hated him,' Hope mused.

'Actually she never stopped loving him. But then there's nowt so queer as folk.'

'Another quote?' There was a blighting bitterness in his words that made her squirm uncomfortably in her seat. Alex the domineering monster was much easier to learn to hate than a man who'd known loneliness and bewilderment as a child.

'Derivative, but every one a gem.'

'Do you stay in contact with your stepmother?'

'Eva?' He looked amused at he thought. 'Not since I bought out her shares in the company.'

'Was she very...?'

'Wicked? Evil and cruel?' He laughed. It was a hard sound. 'I hate to wipe that very fetching light of sympathy from your eyes, Hope, but Eva barely noticed I was there—at least not when I was a child.'

'But you're more friendly now?'

'I didn't mean a special bond developed, Hope. I meant that once I became adult—barely—I became a lot more interesting to her.'

Hope's eyes opened wide with shock 'You don't mean...?'

'I mean Eva has always been a woman who needs constant reassurance that she's attractive. This takes the form of seducing the male of the species.'

'Did she...?' Embarrassed, she looked away from the cynical gleam in his grey eyes.

'I held out—just.' To her surprise he recalled the past with wry humour rather than psychological trauma. 'She was a very attractive woman and I had hormones coming out of my ears. My mother winkled the truth out of me and threatened to inform Dad. I had no more trouble with Eva.'

'Did your father ever find out?'

Alex laughed. 'Dad was too busy pleasing her and trying to influence the people who mattered,' he observed ironically. 'In some ways his preoccupation with Eva took the pressure off me. My father wasn't an easy man to please. After I'd worked for him for a few years I went to university to study design, and from there to Italy. Car design was always my first love.

'Dear God, woman!' he exploded suddenly. 'How the hell do you survive out there with all that empathy?' Looking at the soft sympathy in her eyes infuriated him. Every time he put this woman into a neat compartment she bashed down the bloody walls. It was driving him crazy!

'I don't know what...' she began in a bewildered voice.

'Are you a sucker for every hard luck story? People take sympathy and use it.'

'Are you suggesting I become as hard and impersonal as you?'

'I certainly don't take what people tell me at face-value.'

'You start with the assumption that people are out to mislead you.' This attitude horrified her. 'Caution's OK, but pathological mistrust is ridiculous. I'm not an idiot, Alex, I know most people aren't saints.'

'You think there are *some* saints, then?'

'You can laugh,' she responded, stung by the mockery in his manner. 'But I'll carry on giving people the benefit of the doubt.'

'My God, you're a closet romantic!'

'Am not!'

'Are too.'

Their sudden laughter was strangely companionable. Hope found herself loving the way the laughter lines around his eyes deepened, driving the austerity from his strong face. He looked so approachable it would have been easy to forget...

'How do you know I've not been making up my deprived childhood to get you back into my bed?'

The laughter died abruptly from Hope's face. Talk about being brought back to reality with a bump. 'I'd be surprised that you'd go to so much trouble. I thought your arrogance was so supreme you'd think a nod is all it would take. Besides, what about the barge-pole?'

Alex looked at her blankly.

'The one you wouldn't touch me with,' she reminded him softly.

'Oh, that barge-pole. I haven't forgotten it,' he assured her.

'I'm relieved to hear it. I'll call Adam—he'll pick me up.' She pushed aside her half-eaten toast. Her stomach rebelled just looking at it.

'There's no need. I'm going into town anyway. I'll have to stock up on essentials; the last time we had a major thaw the river broke its banks and I was stranded for three days. I'll just feed the birds first.' He turned and pulled a plate of steak from the fridge. 'Unless you're going to donate Daphne for their breakfast?'

The memory of the cruel beak and talons made Hope shudder. 'Have you got more than one bird?'

'Besides the falcon, a harrier hawk and a barn owl. A friend of mine runs a falconry centre about twenty miles away. He's developed a sanctuary there for sick and injured birds of prey. You'd be surprised how many of those there are. He persuaded me to go hunting with him a while back, and now I've got three of his orphans. A bit like you and Daphne.'

'Hardly. It's cruel.'

'What is? Keeping wild creatures or letting them hunt? Falconry is an ancient sport. The birds would be dead if Jim hadn't taken them in. There is no master-servant relationship with birds of prey—that's what I like about it. They could survive in the wild if they wanted to; they stay because it suits them. Why don't you come and see for yourself?'

He looked surprised he'd made the offer.

'All right.' Curiosity overcame her caution.

The large wooden structures were in the sheltered courtyard of stone outbuildings at the back of the Mill House.

'Watch the ice,' Alex warned as she manoeuvred herself over the slippery cobbles. The snow was fast becoming slushy, but Alex had shovelled pathways through. She watched as he fed the two birds. Their claws looked amazingly large and powerful compared to their light bodies as they tore at their food. They were cruel, but very beautiful.

'You've met Hector—this one's Prospero.' He indicated the smaller bird. 'He's a Merlin.'

'He's so tiny,' she marvelled.

'Here, put this on.' Hope froze in surprise as Alex slid a leather gauntlet on her wrist, but she wasn't too alarmed—both birds were in their pens. 'Lean against me,' he instructed as he took one crutch from her grasp. Her back to him, she automatically leaned against him for support. 'You're cold. You should have put on a coat.'

Hope felt breathless. 'You didn't give me much chance.'

'Now, hold your hand above your head. A bird will

land on the highest point, and you don't want that to be your head.' Hope glanced around in bewilderment as Alex raised her hand.

The size took her by surprise. She'd never seen an owl up close before. The wing span as the bird sailed majestically towards her took her breath away. The creature's snowy plumage put the snow to shame.

'I didn't hear a thing,' she gasped.

'The wings are soft, so she's lethally silent. She's quite heavy,' Alex warned as the talons found a purchase on the leather.

'Where did she come from?' Hope whispered, unable to take her eyes from the magnificent creature.

'She hunts at night, but she nests free—the other side of the house. I'll offer her some food. Are you all right?'

'She's beautiful, Alex,' she whispered in an awed voice.

'I know.' His eyes were not on the half-wild creature.

CHAPTER SEVEN

'Is it done?' Hope opened one eye and looked hopefully at her brother-in-law.

'Quite done,' he confirmed.

'I didn't feel a thing,' she marvelled. Critically she looked down at her pale leg and wriggled her toes. 'That thing makes an awful noise,' she said, grimacing at the small mechanised saw he had just put down.

'You big baby,' he teased. 'I hope you appreciate I don't normally participate in such mundane tasks.'

'I'm honoured,' she responded drily.

'You're a terrible patient. It's obviously genetic.'

'Anna's much worse,' Hope objected.

'As I said, it's genetic. Are you going straight up to London?'

'You can't wait to get rid of me, can you?' she teased.

'That's it, throw my hospitality back in my face.'

Hope grinned. 'Actually, I have packed, but I thought I'd stop off at the farm on the way to see how the work's coming along. I'm reading for the part in the morning.'

'The West End, eh? Are you nervous?'

'Terrified,' she confided, 'but excited.' The idea of working on the stage was thrilling, and it was something she'd always dreamt about. She still couldn't believe that she was being given an opportunity.

'Wouldn't the understudy normally have stepped into the breach when one of the leading ladies' appendix pops?' Adam asked curiously.

'Normally she would, and she is at the moment, but she has got a bad case of morning sickness that wasn't planned for—the sort that lasts twenty-four hours a day by all accounts. She can hardly stand up, let alone play the main support.

'I'm probably making a big mistake here,' she mused out loud. 'Not content with taking over from a successful and highly popular actress, I'm going to muscle in on a company who all know one another. Me! Who has no stage credibility at all! I'm stark, staring mad. At least I know the lines—the local amateur dramatic company did a production in my last year with them.'

'You'll do fine,' Adam said, with the hearty conviction of someone who didn't have to prove the point himself. 'I didn't know you acted back in your teens.'

'Not act, exactly, more scene-shift. I was too tall for all the local male leads by the time I was thirteen, but I did learn everybody's lines in the hope of a flu epidemic,' she confessed wryly. 'I also tripped over a lot.' It's to be hoped I've grown out of *that,* she thought with a strained smile. There was only one way to find out.

Driving her own car again was bliss. It was marvellous not being reliant on anyone else. The morning was crisp and clear, she was young and healthy, and she had the rest of her life to look forward to. Only one thing marred the perfect picture. Try as she might, she couldn't stop the memory of Alex blighting otherwise perfect moments like this.

She parked in the courtyard of the farmhouse. There was only one van parked there. She couldn't remember who was meant to be working today. The new carpets were being fitted on Friday, and she hoped everything was going according to plan. The schedule had been tight.

It had been quite a juggling act, co-ordinating the plumbers, electricians, plasterers and carpenters that were needed to complete the repairs before her parents got back from their cruise. She'd despaired of pulling it off, but just when she'd been tearing out her hair Adam had somehow worked some magic. She suspected the magic had consisted largely of bribery, with a bit of mutual back-scratching thrown in, but by that point she hadn't cared.

The front door was ajar so she went straight in. 'Hello, anyone there?' she called out. There was no reply, so she went up the stairs towards the sound of industry. The plaster from the upper hall ceiling had been pulled down and she could see a pair of boots between the ceiling joists. She stepped over the flex of an electric fire that took the chill of the air. Great, the electrics were back on line. 'That's what I like to see—hard work.'

The figure lowered himself down between the gap in the joists with an impressive display of agility and strength.

'We aim to please.'

Hope felt the colour race to her cheeks. She looked around, more in hope than expectation—no, he was alone. 'Is that the royal we? What are you doing here, Alex?'

'There was a hitch with the joiners.'

'That doesn't answer my question.'

'I'm being neighbourly. What's wrong? Don't you think I'm up to the task?'

'I'm sure you've got better things to do.'

'Actually, I'm glad of the opportunity to get my hands dirty. I don't find anything demeaning in manual labour.' He held out his big square hands palm-up, and Hope felt the shivery, forbidden sensations stir in her belly

'I wasn't suggesting there is.' She tore her eyes away from the sight, only their upward journey did nothing to improve her equilibrium. The green cord shirt he wore had at some point in his labours come unfastened a few inches above his waist. Up to this point she'd managed to avoid looking at the expanse of hair-sprinkled flesh. The strongly delineated muscles of his torso gleamed with a light coating of moisture. The blood was pounding in her ears by the time she reached eye level.

'I sometimes rebel against the schedules, sales targets and interminable meetings,' he continued. 'I play hooky and go and help out on the shop floor. One thing my father insisted on was that I started at the bottom— sweeping floors being the bottom. I learnt every stage of production. I might not be as fast as the men these days, but I can still build one of our cars with my own hands, from start to finish, if push comes to shove. There's nothing to beat the achievement of seeing the results of your labours taking shape under your eyes.' His pride in this capability shone in his face.

'Don't your men feel uncomfortable with you working with them?'

'I've never been much for the "us and them" management style. It's counterproductive and inefficient. Besides, they don't react to my sweaty body the way you do. If they did I might feel uneasy.'

Hope gave a startled gasp as a wave of mortification swept over her. 'Men look—why shouldn't women?' I can't believe I was *that* obvious! 'You've got a good body. There's nothing personal.' She was proud of how cool she sounded.

'Such a liberated lady,' he breathed admiringly. 'And no cast to cramp your style any more.' He looked down at her legs, clad in a fine-denier black. His eyes followed the curve of her calves and the elegant slimness of her thighs until they disappeared beneath the hemline of her leather skirt.

'I'll be able to wear jeans again. It was relief getting

rid of it. Almost as much of a relief as it will be to get rid of you,' she sniped. Being caught ogling like a sex-starved teenager was a major blow to her pride. He had more raw masculinity in his little finger than most men had in their entire bodies.

'You're not satisfied with my work?' He picked up a cloth from the nearby ladder and slowly wiped his hands. The sinews in his forearms corded.

'I'm sure it's exemplary, but it's not…not appropriate for you to be working here,' she said primly.

'Do you mind expanding that a little? I'm a bit slow on the uptake.'

If only he were, life would be a lot simpler. 'If you must know I'm sick of being beholden to you!' she flared thoughtlessly.

'Afraid of the reckoning?' he taunted.

The glitter in his eyes made her wonder just what sort of reckoning he had in mind. Speculation made her stomach tighten with excitement. 'I'm not afraid of you or anything you could do,' she boasted emptily. 'Just leave.' She made a rather grand gesture with her arm.

'I told Adam I'd help.'

'This isn't Adam's house,' she fumed. Short of hiring a crane, there wasn't any way of moving him.

'Neither is it yours,' he pointed out with irritating logic. 'As I said, I'm being neighbourly. Your parents are my neighbours. I've turned over a new leaf.'

'Why?'

He sighed. 'Suspicion in one so young. You're the one who complained I didn't pop round for tea and sympathy.'

'I thought you advocated suspicion.'

'You think everything I do has some dark design, don't you?' he said harshly. 'Maybe I'm just doing it out of love.'

Hearing him joke about it hurt. Pride made her keep her expression noncommittal. 'Perversity, more like—just to irritate me.'

'You think I'd go to that much bother on your account? Besides, if you hadn't turned up unexpectedly today you'd have been none the wiser.'

'I'd have got your bill.'

He grimaced. Her response appeared to irritate him intensely. 'Does everything boil down to that for you—money?'

'What's that supposed to mean?' she asked with dangerous calm. She enjoyed the fruits of her labour, but not even her worst enemy had ever accused her of avarice. 'You expect to be rewarded for what you do. Why should I be any different?'

'It comes down to *what* you do, I suppose,' he drawled, regarding her with a superior sneer that made her teeth grate. 'You take off your clothes to titillate men for money...'

Hope's nostrils flared and her chin went up. 'I have *never* taken off my clothes!' she cried. She'd refused several small fortunes to do just that on numerous occasions. 'I get paid to *wear* clothes, not take them off.'

How dared he make it sound tacky and sordid? She'd be the first to admit she'd been lucky, but she'd worked damned hard, and to hear him casually denigrate what she'd achieved made her furious.

'Don't you find it demeaning to pose provocatively with the sole intention of inflaming men?' He considered her flushed face through narrowed eyes.

'With the sole intention of selling something—usually clothes, and almost always to women!' she contradicted hotly. 'And I don't find anything I've ever done demeaning, with the exception of sleeping with you! I find it hard work.' She gave a wild laugh. 'But then the same could apply to sleeping with you too.'

The venom fell sweetly from her tongue, but looking at the taut, set lines of his face made the hot words shrivel. That one step too far, she silently cursed. I can't stop myself taking it.

'Your memory of the occasion seems to be more vivid than mine.'

'That's a lie,' she gasped. She might be unsure of a lot of things at that moment, but she *knew* she was on solid ground with this.

His lips curved into a wintry, sardonic smile. 'A lie for a lie,' he murmured huskily. 'You started it.'

'I'll take it back if you will,' she offered. A breathless sort of excitement was swirling through her veins. 'It wasn't hard work sleeping with you.'

Satisfaction, hot and hazardous, blazed in his eyes as she made the husky confession.

'I haven't forgotten a single detail of making love to you.' The air almost visibly crackled with static electricity.

Hope cleared her throat noisily. 'Right…humph. It's good to have the record straight.'

'Isn't it? Perhaps we should repeat the experience—if you've got a space in your calendar.'

A nice way to pass the time—that was all it was to him. She knew that already, but it hurt to have her fears so thoroughly confirmed.

'Nice idea, but I'm off to London soon—now, actually. There's nothing to hold me here now.' She bent her knee and flexed her foot to illustrate the healthy state of her injured limb. Just in case he thought anything else had held her here.

'What's in London?' The question was casually curious.

Whilst she hadn't wanted him to give her a hard time, the fact that he'd accepted her departure without a flicker of concern added insult to injury. 'Work—friends. I'm reading for a part in the West End.'

'Hope Lacey conquers the world.'

She didn't want to conquer the world. She wanted to conquer one man. She wanted one man to beg her to stay. She wanted him to declare he couldn't live without her, but that was fantasy time and she knew it. She meant nothing to Alex. Sure, he desired her—but that wasn't enough.

'That's a little premature...maybe next year.'

'This is goodbye, then.'

Don't cry, you idiot, she told herself fiercely. Don't cry! She blinked back the hot sting of unshed tears. 'Bye.'

A hand curled around her forearm as she turned. She spun around.

'Haven't you forgotten something?'

'What...?'

'My bill.'

'Anna has my address,' she began, turning to go once more. She couldn't bear a long, lingering farewell. If she didn't get out of here this instant she'd do something crazy, like say, I love you!

'I don't think we need a middle man.' He jerked her closer.

She gasped as she read the starkly explicit expression in his eyes. 'You're not actually suggesting I sleep with you as payment for services rendered? Out of gratitude! I didn't read any quote that was that ambitious.' She tried to sound amused, but the quiver in her voice spoilt the effect. The unspoken suggestion was outrageous, but outrage wasn't the emotion that was uppermost in her mind as she glared back at him, desperate to hide the fact she had found his suggestion incredibly arousing.

'I'm not suggesting you do anything out of gratitude,' he grated, pulling her securely into his arms. 'Need is the incentive, here—mutual need. I've tried to ignore it, rationalise it, but I can't think straight.' His eyes blazed down at her. 'Do you think I'd actually let you walk out? Just like that! On to pastures new.'

'Actually, Alex, there isn't much you can do to stop me.' The lust and contempt she saw in his eyes made her feel sick. In the midst of her confusion she wasn't able to distinguish the plain fact that he was the target of his own contempt. She stopped trying to twist out of his arms; her struggles only made his steely grip tighten.

'Does it make you feel safe, keeping this distance from your lovers—and I'm not talking miles here? Is it a classic case of safety in numbers?'

'I don't know what you're talking about.' The intensity of the raw emotions emanating from him made her head spin.

'Have you ever paused to think you might find enough with one man?'

It was the very last thing she'd expected to hear him say. *'You?'*

His expression grew grimmer as he misinterpreted her incredulity. 'I don't like sharing the woman in my bed with other men.'

No tender concern; he was just protecting what he saw as his territory. Her fledgling hopes withered and died. 'I'm not your property, Alex Matheson. One night, that's all we had, or will ever have,' she hissed. 'Anyway, you've got some nerve. What about Rebecca?'

'Rebecca's a friend; she's got nothing to do with this.'

'Well, Lloyd is *my* friend.'

'Do you categorise all your ex-lovers as friends, Hope? You must have a lot of "friends."'

'Lloyd is not my ex-lover. He's—'

'Well, for his sake he'd better get transferred to that list in a hurry,' he cut in savagely. 'You don't need him while you've got me.'

'The question is, do I *want* you? I'm sure lots of girls go a bundle on all this machismo, but personally I find this overdose of virility a mite pathetic.' She could see his face through a fog of anger, only it wasn't just anger that clouded her senses; there was a strong element of anticipation and excitement.

'Is that a fact?'

'It is.'

'Then why are you trembling?'

'I…I'm cold,' she whispered huskily.

'If you run out on me, who will keep you warm?'

'I'll buy a hot water bottle,' she suggested weakly. 'God, Alex, this is stupid. Let me go. I know you're not going to force me.'

'You credit me with that much decency? I'm amazed,' he drawled sarcastically. She couldn't take her eyes from the nerve that beat beside his mouth. His mouth—oh, hell! she moaned silently.

'We're not suited. You don't even like me.'

A impatient twist of his head brushed aside her objections. 'We are suited in bed. We don't even need a bed,' he corrected huskily. 'Don't try cold turkey, Hope, it's hell.'

'What option do we have, Alex?'

He placed his hands on either side of her face and drew her lips towards him. Like a man deprived too long of water, he drank in her sweetness.

'God, I've thought about that every second of every day,' he breathed, lifting his head. 'Have you?'

'Oh, yes!' With a small, broken cry she wound her arms about his neck and covered his mouth with her soft, eager lips. 'This is mad.' Mad but marvellous. His coiled strength, the musky male scent of his warm body, the strength of his arousal as she ground her hips against his—how could she deprive herself of these mind-blowing pleasures?

A soft, greedy growl reverberated in his throat as he began to pull at her clothes with impatient hands. She squirmed and wriggled to aid him.

'You're so beautiful, it hurts.' A kiss tinged with the desperation that pervaded them both interspersed his words. His harsh, uneven breathing drowned out her own shallow gasps. 'Do you know what it does to me to look at you?'

'I want...' She almost sobbed the words as her fingers worked diligently at the buckle on his jeans. The strength vanished from her legs at the same moment her skirt slithered to the floor. 'I can't do it!' she wailed in frustration as they sank to their knees. Her desire wasn't gentle or controlled; it was clumsy and eagerly rough. It flowed like a molten river through her veins.

Her arms slid beneath his open shirt. His damp skin was satiny hard and her fingers didn't meet across his magnificent back. She pressed her face to him and placed open-mouthed kisses against his heaving chest. Her teeth tugged against the taut, resistant flesh stretched over his ribcage.

She didn't notice when he reached to drag his coat across the floor to cushion her impact against it. It was a relief to find herself flat on her back. She caught the flapping ends of his shirt-front and tugged him downwards. Together they rolled onto their sides.

Alex pushed aside the lace covering one breast. His eyes were half closed as they ran over the warm, quiv ering flesh. 'Is it the cold doing that?' he asked, watching the pink nipples swell and quiver. 'Or me?'

'You know.' Her fingers curled into the taut contours of his buttocks as his mouth honed in on the tingling area. She looped her thigh over his hips and felt him pulse against the cradle of her pelvis. She yelped as the buckle of his belt pinched her skin.

'What is it?' The skin was drawn tight across his strong bones; his mouth looked fuller and his eyes—oh, God—his eyes made her bones melt.

'Just the belt.'

He ran his fingers down her thigh and moved her knee a little lower. 'Just for a minute,' he promised. One-handed, he slipped the catch.

'No, let me,' she said, covering his hand with her own as he reached for the zipper. She raised herself on her knees to straddle his body, and, tongue caught between her teeth, set about completing the task he'd begun. Alex was watching her from slitted eyes. His chest heaved as if he couldn't draw enough air into his lungs. She could feel the fine tremors that shook his body. She shot him constant sultry glances as she completed her task.

She was so totally absorbed that the sound of her own name being called didn't penetrate the sensual fog that had enveloped them immediately.

'Hope, where are you? I've brought lunch, but I didn't bring enough for two.' The second step always had creaked. Second step—Anna! Hope glanced down at her half-naked body. Her horrified gaze didn't extend as far as Alex's face—she wasn't that brave.

'Oh, God!' Grabbing up her clothes, she ran into the nearest room, which happened to be the bathroom. In a feverish haste she pulled on the garments.

'It's the least I can do, Alex, considering you stepped into the breach like a hero. Hope would have been distraught if we hadn't fixed things up before they were back. For some reason she holds herself personally responsible, but the plumber said that the joint leading into the tank had been leaking for ages. It was already weak. Oh, there you are, Hope. Is the plumbing in good working order now? I was just saying to Alex,' Anna rattled on cheerfully, 'how handy it is to know a man who's good with his hands. What's wrong? What have I said?'

An inarticulate squeak escaped Hope's pale lips. 'Just leave it, Anna.'

Anna unhooked the bulging bag from around her neck. 'Did I come at a bad time? Sorry, I just thought Alex might be hungry, but you obviously had the situation in hand. I'm off—babies are in the car. Must pick up Sam and Nathan from nursery school.'

'No, I'm going myself.' Hope fled.

'Would you excuse me, Anna?'

'Don't mind me...' she began, but she was talking to empty air.

Hope could hear his feet pounding on the stairs, and she gave up all pretence of normality and ran. She'd reached the car before he caught her up.

'Let me go!' She spun around, panting.

Alex caught her by the elbows. 'Calm down,' he commanded firmly. 'What do you think you're doing?'

'I've never been more humiliated in my life.'

'Humiliated that someone knows we were making love?'

She winced at his uncompromising assessment of the situation. 'Do you think she guessed?'

'Well, if she didn't, your little act up there cleared up any doubts. I take it you're ashamed?' His expression was cold and forbidding.

'Who wouldn't be?' she asked shrilly. 'Rolling around on the floor like...like...'

'Animals?'

'If you like,' she said with a touch of defiance. Their primal haste had certainly been something outside her own experience, but then Alex's rampant sensuality was outside her experience too.

'Sorry if I'm not a smooth and civilised lover, Hope, but the fact is you like me the way I am. Crude, coarse and unrefined.'

'You aren't.' She couldn't stop the instinctive protest escaping her lips.

One hand cupped her chin and forced her lowered gaze upwards. 'I'm not what?' His tone demanded an answer. His expression made it clear he was ready to wring the truth from her.

'Any of those things.'

'What am I?' She could feel the tension in him as he waited for her reply.

She didn't need any further prompting. In one way it was a relief to say what she felt. 'Beautiful.' Her tongue curled lovingly around the word. I've started so I might as well finish, she thought recklessly. 'Addictive…' The word emerged, achingly erotic, from her raw throat. 'You've gone quiet all of a sudden.' A hint of belligerence crept into her voice as she looked him straight in the eyes.

His eyes searched her face almost suspiciously. 'You're serious.' He drew in breath hungrily, as though he'd forgotten to breathe.

'Do I look like I'm laughing?' I bare my soul, she thought indignantly, and what do I get? The third degree! 'I'm not exactly enjoying feeling like this.'

'You should be enjoying it. Perhaps we should do something about that.' 'Smug' would have been too mild a word to describe the male satisfaction that was oozing from him.

She swayed slightly as his arms moved to cage her body. Strong arms that made her feel weak and feminine. Dear God, she wondered, where in her subconscious had all these antediluvian fantasies been hiding? One whiff of a pheromone and any thoughts of political correctness went sailing out of the window.

She pressed her lips to the corner of his firm mouth. It would have been a crime to let an opportunity like this slip away. 'What did you have in mind?' She kissed the neglected side of his mouth lingeringly and felt his chest swell.

'How do you feel about orgies?'

'In general I'm fairly open-minded. Are we talking large, communal occasions, here?'

'Smaller, more intimate occasions.' His tongue traced the outline of her open tremulous lips with steady precision. 'One on one, if you get my drift.' His smile was sinfully sensual as her fingers moved to his thick hair. It felt like rich, heavy silk under her fingertips.

'I really have got to go to London, Alex.' If he'd asked her to stay she'd probably have been unprofessional enough to do just that. Only his silence didn't put her resolve to the test. 'If I get this part, things are going to get quite hectic.'

'Where are you staying?'

'With a friend. Female,' she added with a spurt of annoyance. 'So there's no need to look like that.'

'I've got an apartment that you could use.'

Apartment. It smacked too much of being a kept woman, visited by her lover when it suited him. 'I don't think so.' She didn't like the image it conjured up in her mind. She was accepting a lot less than she wanted as it was, and she didn't know for how long she could go on making concessions. She had to draw the line somewhere.

'As you like. I can make it up there at the weekend. It's a date, then.'

Hope nodded. A date had a nice old-fashioned ring to it. What they were arranging was nothing of the sort— more a wild, hedonistic spree of sensual delight. He didn't want or need her love, but for the moment he did want and need her body. Later, she might regret having settled for second best, but at least she'd have something to remember.

She emerged from his savage embrace with the air of a person accustomed to such mind-shattering experiences. 'I'll ring you.'

'That would be advisable.' There was nothing subtle about the warning in his silky words.

'You're late,' Miranda snapped.

Hope stood there, her key still in the lock of her friend's penthouse. 'Tell me about it,' she said wearily. She was bone-tired and close to forming the conclusion that she'd made the worst decision of her life accepting this part. 'You know, they only gave it to me because my name would boost the ticket sales. I have novelty value,' she said bitterly. 'Half the people who come and watch will be hoping I fall flat on my face.'

The self-pity passed right over her friend's head. 'Yeah, yeah. Never mind about that,' she said impatiently.

Miranda was the closest friend she'd made on the modelling circuit. Hope could see that she was agog. She had fair skin that went with a cloud of red hair. Her complexion always reflected her emotions, and right now she was pink with excitement.

'What's happened?'

'He's been waiting three hours for you.' It was only at times like this that her normally accentless English betrayed her Norwegian origins. 'Dark hair, big—very big.' She licked her lips reflectively. 'The sort of body that looks better without clothes on.' She gave a crow of delight as Hope's tell-tale blush confirmed her theory. 'I knew I was right. Clothes can't hide a body like that. You know, I'm tired of skinny, pretty boys. Tell me, do you think he'd pose for my life class?' she enquired in all seriousness. 'He could really get my artistic juices flowing.'

'If you ask him I'll kill you!' Art was Miranda's latest craze; last month it had been hang-gliding.

'Well, if you feel like that I won't,' she responded with obvious regret. She half closed her eyes and a dreamy look came over her face. 'I can just imagine him…'

'Don't!' Hope said tartly. She thought it was about time she drew this speculation to a close.

Her friend's hand on her arm stilled her impetuous entry into the open-plan living area. 'He's angry.'

'What?'

'Under the charm.' She wrapped her arms around her slim body and sighed deeply. 'It's so refreshing to meet a really intelligent man.'

'Just what have you two been talking about?' Hope asked sharply. It seemed to her that it wasn't Alex's intelligence that her friend had been drooling over.

'He's angry, Hope—with you, I think.'

'Well, don't look at me. It's par for the course. He's always angry at me for something or other. I could spend a week in a retreat in Outer Mongolia and I'd still do something to aggravate the man!'

Miranda's green eyes grew round as they rested on Hope's face. 'I never thought I'd live to see the day!'

'Don't talk in riddles,' Hope responded crossly.

'I shall go to bed.'

'Not before time,' Hope shouted after her.

'Alex.' He stood with his back to her. Alex had a magnificent back. Amazing how a rear view could give such a clear impression of disposition. Even without Miranda's warning, she'd have known he was in a right royal fury.

'What time do you call this?' He spun around.

Hope took her time examining the slender watch about her wrist before replying. 'One-thirty.'

'And what have you been doing? Or is that a silly question?'

'Pompous doesn't suit you, Alex, but then I'm sure you know that. Actually—though it's none of your business—I've been working my butt off. You can see if you like,' she offered generously. She craned her head to get a view of her rear, clad in a pair of skin-tight jeans that clung lovingly to long lines of her legs.

'At one-thirty!' He watched as she pulled off the short leather jacket she wore. The skinny rib polo neck clung to her curves like a second skin. At one time he'd convinced himself she was unaware of how provocative clothes like that were when they covered a body like hers. That had been before he'd been forced to face a few unpalatable facts.

'Actually, we stopped at midnight for refreshments.'

'I just bet you did,' he drawled. 'Who's we?'

'Jonah—Jonah Cromwell, the director—and me.'

'Cosy.'

'I didn't know I had a curfew.'

'Did you share the joke with him?'

She sighed. 'I'm tired, Alex, thoroughly fed-up and on the verge of hysteria. So if all this nonsense is leading somewhere, get to the point!'

'This,' he said, flinging a rolled-up newspaper at her, 'is the point!'

'Oh, is that all?' She slumped into the stylish red leather and chrome chair that hadn't been created with the human spine in mind. The full story of Lloyd and Shirley had been told in inside-colour-spread splendour in a Saturday supplement. 'I thought you'd be pleased.'

'Pleased? Pleased to be made a total fool of?'

She blinked. This wasn't the response she'd been anticipating. 'You were a bit silly, weren't you?' The perverse temptation to taunt a tiger was irresistible in her present frame of mind.

'You knew I was half-insane, thinking of you with that man.' His lip curled in a savage snarl as he bit out the word. 'You knew I half expected you to up and run when he crooked his finger. Did you get a kick out seeing me want to throttle the life out of the bastard? Do you like seeing men make fools of themselves over you?'

The extent of his unreasoning fury hit her for the first time. 'I tried to tell—' she began, but Alex wasn't here to hear excuses.

'You made yourself the laughing stock of the country for that man.'

'The entire population doesn't treat the tabloids as gospel. I was helping out a friend.'

'Some friend. Some *casual* favour.'

'Come on, Alex, you can't have it both ways. A second ago you were angry that Lloyd *wasn't* my lover. Now you're mad because you think we're tied together by some invisible bond of eternal friendship. If I'm going to be reviled, I'd like to know what for, exactly.'

'You want it straight? Fine!' His lips thinned to a grim line of distaste. He made a supreme effort to control his erratic breathing. 'I think you enjoyed seeing me go through hell thinking of you in his arms—his hands all over you.'

He closed his eyes, as though seeing a particularly terrible vision. He couldn't forget all the hours he'd spent agonising over his obsessive interest in a woman too young for him—unsuitable in every way. The way she'd flaunted her apparent affair with a married man should have put her out of bounds. He'd made a big production of saying just that. Five minutes later he'd been panting to rationalise his change of heart. No wonder she'd let him dangle; she had enjoyed the spectacle of him making a clown of himself. At my age, he thought with contempt, I ought to know better.

'You wouldn't listen.'

Some things didn't change.

He continued in a driven voice, 'It was more fun seeing me come into line, wasn't it? You knew I'd never hold out. You didn't tell me the truth because you got a kick out of it.'

'That's not true,' she gasped. Did he actually think she was capable of playing such sordid games?

'And you thought I'd come crawling to you, overcome with remorse, when the truth finally came out.' Her guilty flush at the arbitrary sliver of truth made his eyes narrow. 'You know what I think? I think you'd have to owe someone big time to place your reputation on the line. I think there's more between you and Elliot than meets the eye. What did he promise you?'

'Haven't you ever helped out a friend, Alex?'

Her quiet question seemed to shake him. 'Are you trying to suggest you had no ulterior motive?' He resurrected his blighting scorn without any visible effort. 'You couldn't be straight if you tried, Hope. Has anything you've ever said to me been the truth?'

Hope got to her feet. Being blasted by this much raw

contempt was a shattering experience. She was shaking with reaction. Later she might cry, but right now she was way past that form of release.

'I wanted to explain to you, Alex, but I couldn't get past that wall of cynicism you've erected. This isn't about me, is it? It's about you being human and fallible. You can't take not being in control.'

'If there's a control freak here, it's not me.'

What little control Hope had had over her temper snapped completely at this point. 'You know what I think, Alex? I think you're disappointed I'm not the bad girl you had me pegged as. I think naughty girls get you turned on, and the idea you could force me to give up Lloyd made you feel like a really big man.'

'You don't really imagine I *need* that sort of prurient stimulation?' He shook his head in shocked disbelief.

'Oh, dear!' she trilled, covering her mouth with her hand. 'Have I insulted your virility? Tough!' She spat the word out and her eyes grew hard. 'You can sail in here and throw every vile insult that your sordid little mind can conjure up. But if I draw what is a perfectly logical conclusion, you're offended. I'd say that about sums up perfectly what passes for our relationship.'

'Then possibly now is the time to end what obviously disgusts you.' Nostrils flared, eyes like ice chips, he managed to give the impression of looking down on her even though they were eye to eye.

'Sounds good to me.' She rocked on her heels and smiled.

'Fine!'

Miranda discovered her half an hour later, standing still as a statue staring out of the window blindly at the glittering lights. Her soft words of sympathy opened the floodgates.

Amidst the storm Hope heard her friend say soothingly, 'I've got a little mask I keep in the fridge that works wonders for puffy eyes.' She wondered if there was anything there for a broken—no, bruised heart. 'Broken' implied the damage was irreparable. She couldn't contemplate that possibility.

CHAPTER EIGHT

'I've taken the liberty of placing you in one of the alcoves, sir. The large party is a little boisterous—an engagement, I believe.'

'Scotch, no ice, please,' Jonathan said as he took his seat. 'Mineral water, Hope?'

'No, I'll have the same as you. Make it a double.'

Jonathan looked surprised, but nodded at the waiter. 'Never seen you drink anything but wine before, Lacey, love. Are you feeling OK? You look a bit pale. Not anything catching, is it?'

'Don't worry, Jon, you're safe.'

'It's you I was concerned about, love.'

Hope threw her agent an ironic look which failed to penetrate his armour-plated skin. 'Do you mind if we swop seats? I feel a bit on display here.' This wasn't much of an excuse; between the greenery and the strategically placed screens, she was scarcely visible from the main dining area.

Jonathan got obligingly to his feet. 'You'll never learn. If you've got, it, love, flaunt it.' He looked expectantly at her and she smiled obligingly. It was one of his favourite sayings and he always wheeled it out as though it was a witty and original gem.

'You'll never guess who's over there,' he said as he took her seat.

'No, who?' she asked brightly.

'That big guy who gave me the run-around with that compensation deal. You fell down that hole in his factory. You know, love, I never could understand what you were doing there.' He chuckled reminiscently and picked up the menu. 'He wasn't as clever as I thought. Apparently there were signs all over saying, "No admittance to the public". We'd never have got a penny out of him if we'd gone to court.'

'Aren't I lucky my agent's so clever?'

'Want to go over and say hello?'

Hope stared at him in horror. 'Are you *mad*?'

Jonathan shrugged. 'I feel quite mellow about the whole thing. We'd be quids in if you hadn't insisted on giving the whole bundle to charity, Lacey.'

Hope took a deep swallow of the whisky. 'Leave it, Jon.'

Her agent contented himself with an unhappy mutter. He cast his eyes down the expensive menu. 'Is this on you?'

'It would seem so,' Hope said drily.

'In that case...'

•

'Are you going to eat that?' Jon looked at the untouched salmon on her plate, floating in an interesting-looking dill sauce.

'Feel free,' she said, leaning back in her seat. Jon had already polished off his own meal and she wondered idly where he put all the calories. He was a thirty-something man with a thin, wiry frame. When he wasn't eating he was talking, and sometimes he did both simultaneously, which didn't make him her favourite dining companion. Hope found him exhausting company at any time. Only tonight she was quite glad of his chatter.

'You can't afford to sit back on your laurels, Hope,' he observed with his mouth full. 'People forget quickly. You want to move ahead while your success is still fresh in people's minds.'

'I won't,' she agreed vaguely, or should that have been, I will? she wondered. Strange how empty success was. She'd always thought it was an end in itself. But she wanted someone to share her pleasure—not just her family, someone special, someone of her own. Was that so much to ask? The gaping hole in her life wasn't empty; it was filled with pain.

'In the good old days she'd have been convalescing for months with a burst appendix, not a measly three weeks.'

Hope's attention strayed as the sound of laughter from across the room rang out. It made her wince. Her first instincts when she'd seen Alex, the instant she'd stepped over the threshold of the exclusive restaurant, had been to turn tail and run.

He stood out in a party of a dozen or so. The sight of his strong profile and dark head of hair had been like a band of steel tightening around her chest. It had given the momentary impression of suffocation. Making it to the table had been more exhausting than running a marathon. That the pain she was experiencing was phantom made it no less real.

Rebecca had been seated on his right, a vibrant, glowing Rebecca, and Alex had had her hand pressed to his lips as everyone raised their glasses. The waiter's words had only confirmed her suspicions. The tableau said everything she needed to know.

Well, it hadn't taken him long to get over her, she reflected, staring at the bottom of her glass broodingly. Jonathan's only comment had been, 'You're paying,' when she'd ordered the second bottle, but she'd seen he was surprised.

'You're not a happy drunk, are you?' Her companion's voice interrupted her gloomy reverie.

'I'm not drunk.' More's the pity, she thought, with a fresh spurt of self-pity. 'But the night's still young.'

Jonathan frowned. Lacey had never been one of the clients he'd had to get tough with over burning the candle at both ends. He hoped she wasn't going to go crazy

on him. There was a worrying wildness about the way
she was looking tonight.

'Champagne—we didn't order champagne,' Hope
said as the waiter placed a bucket on the table.

Jonathan looked at the label. 'Good stuff,' he said,
impressed.

'With the compliments of the party over there.' The
waiter inclined his head towards the centre of the room.

'Well, that's very decent of the man, I must say.'
Jonathan waved his class cheerfully towards the laughing group.

'Take it back!'

Jonathan gaped at Hope. 'Don't be crazy; this is really
excellent.' He twisted the bottle in its chilled bed.

'I wouldn't take a crumb off that man if I was starving.'

The viciousness in her low, intense voice made
Jonathan stare. 'Well, I can understand he's not your
favourite person. It must have been bloody painful,
breaking your leg and everything—anyone would resent
it. But it's not as if he pushed you down personally, is
it?'

'Take it away!'

'Hell, Lacey, there's no need to make a scene.'

'If I want to make a scene, I will.' He wasn't content
with ruining her life, he wanted to rub her nose in his
happiness. He was a heartless swine! And she hated him.

The object of her hate materialised at her side. 'Is
there a problem with the champagne?'

She smelt him before she actually heard him. That
light, spicy stuff he wore underlaid by a more subtle
male fragrance that was as unique as a fingerprint. It was
horrifying to find her senses so finely attuned to him.
And, why had she expected he'd look different? It had
only been two weeks. Each strong feature was the way

she remembered it. Memory hadn't exaggerated his presence or pure, unadulterated sexiness.

'Alex, what a surprise. I'm afraid I don't like champagne.' She didn't sound afraid; she sounded glad she could reject his generosity. It was strange to look at his hands and think how well they knew her body. The pain of loss slid through the barrier of her anger and it was devastating.

'I do,' Jonathan retorted lightly.

Alex flicked him one dismissive look before turning his attention to Hope. 'Rebecca saw you come in.'

'Did you?'

His jaw tightened. 'I'm sure *everyone* saw your entrance.' There was no hip-swaying affectation for Hope. She walked with a long-legged, confident stride that had stretched the fabric of her long gown to the limit. His narrowed eyes ran over the strapless midnight-blue gown. The diamond clip in her upswept hair matched the sparkling gems in her ears. She was classically sexy.

A sudden laugh drew Alex's attention to her companion. 'She doesn't notice that everyone stares,' Jonathan murmured authoritatively. 'Hard to believe, I know, but true,' he added, in face of the hard scepticism on the older man's face.

'Do you mind?' Hope glared at Jonathan.

'Rebecca wants everyone to share her happiness.'

'It was her idea?'

One slanted brow shot upwards, and his lips twisted in a mocking smile. 'You thought it was from me?'

'I didn't even know you were here.' She kicked Jon under the table just in case he was going to open his big mouth at the wrong moment. How dared they discuss her as though she wasn't in the room?

'Forgotten my name too, have you?' He didn't bother to hide his scepticism.

'I'm working on that.

'Thank Rebecca for the champagne and wish her all the best in the future.' Let no one say I don't have very nice manners.

'Hope you'll both be very happy.' Jon rubbed his shin and reached for the bottle before anyone changed their mind. 'Join us for a toast and we'll drink to your future. What? What have I done now?' he asked with an injured expression as Hope looked daggers at him.

Alex had turned back in the act of moving away. 'You'll drink to *my* future?' A curious expression had entered his eyes.

'I'll toast anyone who buys me a drink.'

'Based on past experience, your honesty is surprising.'

'That was business. No hard feelings.' Jon patted the dark sleeve of Alex's suit, then regretted the casual intimacy under the narrow-eyed stare of the older man's slatey eyes.

'Will *you* drink to my future, Hope?'

Hope swallowed the painful constriction in her throat. The thudding in her temples increased in tempo. She could feel his eyes coldly analysing every shift of expression on her face. The flicker of an eyelash, the tilt of her chin.

'I hope you get everything you deserve from life.' Nicely translated it came out as, Rot in hell, and she was sure from Alex's expression that he understood every word.

Why did I go and do that? she wondered. I'm not supposed to give a damn either way. Her languid scorn was a joy to behold—she'd practised it enough. Now was not the time for improvisation. Though in her mental rehearsals Alex hadn't been about to marry another woman, so she did have some excuse for straying from the script.

'I'm touched.' His gesture resulted in a chair being brought promptly. 'I will have that drink with you.'

His knees touched hers beneath the table and Hope drew back as if stung. Her cool façade had crumbled ignominiously at the slight, possibly deliberate physical contact. Angry, she smoothed invisible wrinkles from the moulded bodice of her dress. When she looked up Alex's eyes were fixed on the exposed creamy cleavage. The light boning did make the best of her assets.

'We wouldn't want to keep you from your own party.' She hated herself for responding to the burning hunger in his glance.

'Rebecca can afford to be generous tonight.'

His smug certainty grated on Hope. Did he know each word was like a poisoned dart? 'I'd be worried if my future husband ogled other women's breasts the way you do.' I sound like a spiteful bitch, she realised in dismay.

'Oh, hell,' Jonathan groaned quietly as he choked on the excellent champagne. So *that* was what Lacey had been doing in the country.

'If you shove them in a man's face he doesn't have much choice but to look, sweetheart,' he drawled.

Hope stiffened with outrage—shove them! 'In other words, a woman who doesn't hide her body in a sack is asking for it,' she breathed wrathfully.

'It's men's nature to look, and your body would still be an invitation in a sack.'

'Amen to that,' Jonathan breathed.

'Don't you *dare* side with him! He's accusing me of being a vamp.'

'Only after you accused me of being a lecher,' Alex pointed out pedantically.

'I'm going to the little boys' room.' Jonathan gave the almost full bottle a wistful glance before he left.

Alex watched the younger man retreat with an expression of scorn. 'He's going to run out on you.'

'I know,' she said tolerantly.

'Why do you put up with him? He's a creep.'

'He's a very good agent.' 'Creep' was being a little hard. 'And there's no possibility of him falling in love with me,' she murmured hazily.

Alex's glance sharpened—no, she couldn't be, he decided. There wasn't even the suspicion of a slur to mar her clear diction. 'Perhaps we should be toasting your success.'

'You heard about that, then?' She tried to put pleasure into her lack-lustre response.

'I saw it.'

His words shocked her. The idea of Alex out there one night in the darkness watching her sent a secret shiver down her spine. 'I'm glad I didn't know,' she confessed unthinkingly. For some reason words seemed to be popping unbidden into her mouth.

'Why?' He filled her glass, but left his own empty.

'An audience should be anonymous.' How could she have forgotten who she was and thrown herself into a characterisation if she'd known he was there? She'd have frozen; he made her too aware of exactly who she was. 'So—marriage.' She emptied her glass in one gulp and swirled the slender-stemmed goblet in a wide arc.

As Alex ducked to avoid a collision with his head it occurred to him that despite her controlled speech the lady really was well and truly drunk. 'Yes, indeed, marriage. Are we talking in general here, or...?'

'Yours. Yours and Rebecca's. You've never done it before?'

'Not so as I recall.'

'She's nice.'

'I think so.'

'Then I hope you'll be very happy.' She felt a saintly glow of self-sacrifice as she earnestly told him this. 'When's the wedding?'

'Next week.'

She swallowed hard and looked straight head. Well,

that should put a stop to her romantic daydreams. Nothing like the brutal truth to wake a girl up to the futility of fantasies.

'I don't suppose there's much point waiting when you already know one another.'

'That's what Rebecca says.'

'Marriage is pretty serious.'

'It is. Until very recently I didn't think I'd ever marry.'

'Why not?' Her deep blue eyes were fixed with reluctant fascination on his face.

'Like my father, I'm pretty selfish. Selfish men make hellish husbands. I'd hate to put a woman through what my mother suffered at his hands.'

'But you've changed your mind?'

'Someone changed it for me.'

Rebecca. Hope wanted to throw herself on the floor and weep. Instead she did the mature thing and had another drink.

'Do you think you should have any more of that?' he asked, watching her fill the glass with a less than steady hand.

'Oh, I was lying when I said I didn't like it. I didn't like the whisky, though.' She plonked her elbows on the table and rested her chin in her cupped hands. 'It tastes really disgusting.'

'Why did you have it, then?'

'I wanted to experiment. I know people who enjoy being tipsy.' Alex wasn't usually this slow on the uptake; she felt quite disappointed in him.

'Tipsy happened half a bottle ago, Hope. In my experience it's usually safer to experiment in private, with a small audience. People react differently to alcohol, and you're entering the maudlin stage. Your escort departed at the bolshie stage.'

'Maudlin is pathetic,' she protested rather loudly. 'I am *never* pathetic; it's humiliating. Is it warm in here?'

'It's getting warmer,' he said softly as she plucked fretfully at the plunging neckline of her gown. 'How does that thing stay up?' He blinked hard to banish the image of the silky fabric sliding lower to reveal— The muscles in his throat worked hard as he swallowed.

Hope patted the side of her nose and looked mysterious. 'Trade secret. Is that Rebecca coming over here?' She craned her neck to look over his shoulder. 'Oh, God,' she moaned gloomily, 'I'll have to be *nice* to her.'

Alex's lips twitched. 'Don't worry, I'll deal with it.'

She swopped seats so she could see Alex meet Rebecca a few feet away. She couldn't hear what they were saying, but Rebecca looked over to her several times and even returned the waves Hope sent in her direction. She smiled and nodded a lot before going back to her seat.

'I don't suppose your beau paid the bill?' Alex asked.

'Nope,' Hope replied, laying her head on her folded arms.

'Don't go to sleep yet.'

'God, you're so bossy. Put that card away,' she said crossly as she saw him signing for the meal. 'I'm an independent woman of means.'

'You're sloshed.'

'I knew there was something wrong.' She stared owlishly at him. 'What should I do?' She gazed trustingly up at him.

He closed his eyes and she distinctly heard him mutter something about strength. 'I'm taking you home.'

'Rebecca wouldn't like that,' she told him, wagging her finger at him.

'She doesn't mind. Call it a loan.'

'If you ask me,' she said darkly, 'she should be more careful with her possessions. I would be.'

* * *

'Are you still staying with the lovely Miranda?' Alex asked as he finally managed to slide her into the back seat of a cab.

'Did you fancy her, then? She fancied you.'

'That's very gratifying,' Alex said, giving the address to the driver and climbing in beside her.

'I shouldn't think anyone noticed I'm drunk. I think we were very un...unobtrusive.' She placed her head on Alex's shoulder and closed her eyes. The world started to spin in a nauseating fashion so she opened them again. 'I don't know why you made such a fuss about my ear-ring. People were staring.' She touched the earlobe of her naked ear.

'You're very casual about a small fortune.'

'Don't be silly,' she said, rubbing a finger along the strong line of his jaw. 'They're not real. I can't believe you think I'd spend a fortune on diamonds,' she said incredulously. 'They're paste.' She tugged off the other one. 'Next you'll be saying this is real animal fur.' She touched the collar of her jacket. 'You really don't know me very well, do you? I'm not really into *things*.'

Alex looked at the top of her head with an expression that softened his harsh features. 'I'm beginning to think you're right.'

'That was quite a rock Rebecca was wearing.'

'You saw that from across the room?'

'I'm a woman, Alex. Women notice these things. Some people might call it tasteless and ostentatious.'

'Not you, of course.'

'That would catty,' she agreed virtuously. 'She obviously thinks diamonds are a girl's best friend.'

'Who do you think should be a girl's best friend, Hope?'

'A lover would be nice, don't you think?' she murmured, with a sleepy smile that made Alex catch his breath sharply.

* * *

'There's no point ringing—Miranda's in Cairo,' she said as Alex shifted her weight to reach the intercom. 'The lifts are over there,' she added, swinging her legs as he hitched her a little higher. 'You can put me down now. My leg's all better.' She lifted the hem of her skirt above her knees to illustrate the point. 'It was only that little step I couldn't quite get the hang of. You're very strong, aren't you?' she observed feeling his bulging bicep. 'You've got beautiful muscles.'

'If the lift's not working, don't worry—you'll walk.' There was a hint of desperation in Alex's tone and it wasn't directly connected with her weight.

'This isn't the sort of building that has out of order lifts, Alex.' It wasn't, but the lift did have other passengers, who smiled politely and looked in the other direction as she crooned softly in his ear and let his hair slide over her delving fingers.

When they eventually reached their destination Alex placed her on her feet, but stood ready to catch her should the need arise.

'Promise me one thing.'

'Anything,' she promised happily, wrapping her arms around his neck.

'Never do a musical.' The barely recognisable strains of a top ten hit were still echoing in his ears.

'Why would I do that, silly? I'm tone deaf.' She walked with immense care to the opposite side of the room and sank gracefully into the designer sofa. 'Miranda says this is an investment,' she observed, looking with disapproval at the geometric upholstery. 'I hate it. Are you going back to Rebecca now?'

'I'm making you coffee—lots of it—now.' When he returned a few minutes later Hope was snoring quietly, her head uncomfortably lolling forward on her chest.

Alex stood there watching her silently for several minutes. His rugged exterior hid a sensitivity and emotional depth that for one unguarded moment was visible in the twisted smile on his lips. The attempts he made to rouse her were greeted with cross admonitions to 'leave me alone.'

Amnesia was scary. The taste in her mouth was metallic and disgusting. The blue designer gown she'd worn last night was tidily arranged over the chair. She took comfort in the sight, reasoning she couldn't have been *that* bad if she'd taken such care. She peeped under the covers and saw she was only wearing the silky pants she'd worn last night.

The movement of the king-sized water bed as she got out affected her delicate stomach badly. She pushed a hand through her tangled hair and frowned at her reflection in the mirror. She belted a thin thigh-length robe around her waist and headed for the bathroom. Cold water splashed on her face had a bracing effect, and her mouth felt a little less disgusting after she'd cleaned her teeth.

For some strange reason she kept smelling fresh coffee. Perhaps that was some undiscovered side effect of a hangover. Because a hangover was what she had. For the first and, if she had anything to say about it, last time in her life.

Coffee was a good idea, though, she decided, heading in the direction of the kitchen. Miranda had a glossy designer kitchen with every gadget known to man, but usually no food. Hope had bought her own coffee; she couldn't stomach the evil herbal tea that Miranda drank by the gallon. She wished she hadn't thought about her stomach...

She stepped from the bedroom directly into the living area at the same moment someone else stepped out of the kitchen.

'Oh, my God!' she gasped, freezing. Alex was rub-

bing his still wet hair with a towel; his white shirt open
to the waist revealing his broad chest in all its glory.
He'd been wearing that shirt last night. *Last night!* She
groaned. 'How could you?' she wailed. 'I was drunk.'

'As a skunk,' he agreed cheerfully. 'How could I
what, Hope? Do you want coffee. I'd offer you a good
old-fashioned fry-up,' he said cruelly, 'except I can only
find balsamic vinegar, herbal tea and brioches in the
kitchen. The brioches are stale.'

'They were fresh yesterday.' Or had it been the day
before? Her appetite hadn't been up to much lately.
'You're getting married,' she said suddenly. She'd discovered the reason for that nebulous feeling of doom
and disaster she'd been experiencing ever since she'd
woken.

'Am I to infer from that wild look there are some gaps
in your memory?'

'I don't think I want to remember.' Her eyes watched
with horrified fascination as the muscles glided and
bunched under his olive-toned skin when he looped the
towel about his neck.

'You didn't get up on the tables or anything.'

Hope glared at him with loathing. 'It's not my *public*
performance I'm worried about.' She sat down before
her legs folded. 'Do you mind?' Her eyes flashed and
she tugged her gown a few centimetres lower as she
caught the direction of his gaze.

'Last night you weren't so modest.'

'I don't want to hear about last night. I don't know
how you can stand there looking so smug. You're about
to marry another woman.' Her hand went to her mouth
as a bit more of the previous evening slipped back into
place. 'Next week!' she squeaked. 'You're a faithless,
lying swine. How dare you laugh?' Was there no end to
his iniquities?

'You're assuming that you're irresistible.'

'Are you trying to tell me we didn't...?'

Head on one side, he regarded her with an expression of exaggerated amazement to match her own. 'Amazing as it might seem to you, I prefer my women conscious. Snoring is a big turn-off too,' he reflected thoughtfully.

Hope could feel the tide of warm colour wash over her skin. 'Well, why didn't you say so straight away?'

'I didn't want to spoil your righteous indignation. Last night you were a kitten and this morning a dragon. The transformation is fascinating.'

Kitten? What did he mean, kitten? It sounded pretty damn alarming to her. 'What was I supposed to think? I was stark naked...'

'Almost.'

'Well, if you're going to be pedantic—' she began. 'How did you know that?' she asked with the return of suspicion.

'I undressed you when I carried you to bed. I didn't want you to suffocate in the night. That blue thing looked pretty tight to me.'

The thought of him undressing her made the downy hairs on the nape of her neck stand on end. 'What the hell are you still doing here? If you didn't—' She winced. Her voice was high, bordering on shrill.

'Have my wicked way with you? No, Hope, those are the bits you dreamed. I thought you might be ill during the night.'

The implication that her dreams were X-rated and included him made her squirm uncomfortably. Hopefully it was a wild guess. The idea that under the influence she'd confided the contents of the vivid dreams she'd been experiencing just lately made her grow cold with horror. 'Well, I wasn't!' she snapped back ungratefully. 'Was I?' Her eyes clouded with dismay. Wasn't her humiliation bad enough without that?

'No, you weren't. You look terrible this morning, though. What do you usually take after a bender?'

'I wouldn't know. That was my first.' And last, she thought, lifting her hand to her throbbing head. 'Unless you count the bottle of cider we drank in the barn when we were thirteen.'

'What made you start last night?'

She eyed him resentfully. *What does he expect me to say? I found out you were marrying someone else and I wanted to dull the pain! God, I probably already told him.* Desperately she tried to piece together the fragmented memories of the previous evening. It would help if she knew what indiscretions had passed her lips…

'Won't Rebecca wonder where you are?'

'She knows where I am.'

'She must trust you.' Her lips quivered slightly and she firmly clamped them together.

'I'll get you coffee.'

'I am thirsty.'

'Dehydration. Alcohol plays havoc with your electrolyte balance.' He sounded knowledgeable on the subject, but Hope didn't understand or care.

The bitter aroma of the coffee curled in her nostrils as she sipped the scalding liquid. 'Should I apologise for my behaviour last night?'

She tried to make it sound as if his reply wasn't that important. She was painfully sober now, and she knew, as desperate as she was to have him love her, she couldn't make it obvious. In fact, it was imperative she hid it! Last night the barriers had been down. She didn't like to contemplate what she might have revealed then.

'You were charming last night. If you discount the singing.'

Hope tried to detect any sign of deceit on his face. Perhaps he was tactfully sparing her blushes. He never had done so before, she reminded herself. 'I don't sing.

I was only in the choir to make up numbers at school—
I had to mime.'

'A very wise decision on someone's part.'

'What happened to Jon? Why didn't he bring me
home?'

'He anticipated a scene.'

She knew Jonathan; she didn't need any further explanations. 'What happened to the scene?'

'I averted it.'

'When I've got more than your word to go on I might
even say thank you.'

Alex ignored the chrome chair and squatted down on
his haunches. 'Tell me, why is not being in love with
you such an important pre-requisite to being your
agent?'

'What makes you think that?' She shot him a shocked
look.

'Just something you said,' he said casually.

My first agent, Hugh—our relationship strayed away
from the purely professional. Which was fine at first, but
he…'

'Fell in love with you?'

Hope nodded. She'd been shocked when he'd asked
her to marry him and move to the East Coast. 'It got
messy.'

'You didn't love him?'

She raised her sad eyes to his face. 'He accused me
of using him. I think I was, in a way. I was only nineteen
and a long way from home. I did rely on him a lot.'

'Some people might say he took advantage of you.'

'Oh, no, it wasn't like that. He was my friend. Perhaps
he will be again one day.'

Alex's expression seemed to indicate he didn't think
much of this idea. 'Do you defend all your friends?'

'If the need arises, I hope so.'

'Hope.' There was urgency in his voice as he fell forward onto his knees. 'There's something I have to tell—'

Hope was experiencing urgency of her own. 'I'm going to be ill,' she announced, jumping to her feet. Hand over her mouth, she fled to the bathroom, leaving him watching her with an expression of seething frustration on his face.

When she returned, pale, but feeling slightly less fragile, the room was full of people—at least that was the way it seemed to her. Her dazed eyes located Miranda standing next to Alex. She was wearing transparent baggy harem-style trousers, a beaded purple top that revealed a large portion of her midriff and a scarf wrapped turban-style around her head.

'Disaster!' she said dramatically, surging forward with her hand still firmly attached to Alex's arm. 'There was a terrorist bomb in the hotel. Chaos! The noise, dust, sirens. We were all packed off early. I invited everyone back for a bite to eat—but wouldn't you know it? There's no food. I've sent out for some breakfast. Do you want...?'

'I've already eaten,' Hope said hastily. 'Was anyone hurt?'

'Fortunately not, but it really got the adrenaline flowing. I think someone called it the old blitz spirit, whatever that is. And you, how's your adrenaline doing?' She slid a sly look at Alex.

'I was just congratulating Alex on his engagement.'

The humour died from Miranda's face. 'Isn't that nice?' Her green eyes were clouded with sympathy. 'Tell me, Alex, have you ever thought of posing? I've joined this art class and—'

'Thanks for the offer,' Alex said with admirable composure. 'But I've a pretty heavy schedule.'

'Well, if you change your mind.'

'She means well,' Hope said as Miranda drifted away.

'I'm flattered.' A steely expression of determination entered his eyes. 'This isn't what I had in mind, but we really should talk.'

'Actually, I think I'll go back to my bed before one of this lot bags it. I'm feeling a bit...' She shrugged. 'I know its self-induced, but...'

'You don't have to explain. I've been there. I've got a busy week, but...'

'I expect you're trying to tidy loose ends. Are you going on a honeymoon?' she asked brightly.

'About that, Hope...'

She hit out at the hand which was extended towards her. 'Oh, God!' she burst out, her self-control deserting her. 'Spare me the details!' Aware that her explosion had coincided with a lull in the general conversation, she wanted to sink through the floor. Instead she ran to her bedroom and locked the door.

CHAPTER NINE

BEING picked up at the airport by Sam Rourke had impressed her fellow models, who weren't aware of the family connection. Several flashbulbs went off as they left the terminal. Supermodels and Hollywood actors always made good copy, and in tandem they were irresistible. Her sister was waiting in the car and she drove swiftly off once the two passengers had got in.

'Good flight, Hope?'

'I've known worse.' Hope leaned forward to affectionately press a kiss to her sister's cheek before she belted herself into the back of the car. 'Well, there's no need to ask if you two had a good time?' Above and beyond her golden tan, Lindy had a definite glow.

The back of her sister's neck went a deep shade of carnation-pink as she drove, but her new husband grinned, unperturbed by the remark.

'You were cutting it fine, godmother,' Sam remarked. Hope had the impression his light, teasing remark was intended to take the attention off his wife, though she couldn't see why. It would seem Sam was getting incredibly protective.

'I prefer to call it split-second timing.'

She'd jumped at the unexpected offer of a fashion shoot in Colorado. Being several thousand miles away when Alex was tying the knot with Rebecca seemed like too good an opportunity to miss. 'I said I wouldn't miss the christening, and here I am. Besides, I promised Mum and Dad I'd spend Christmas at home this year. It's the first time in ages we've all been together. Not that it'll be the same as old times.' She knew that this evolution

165

was natural—both her sisters were married now—but all the same a hint of wistfulness entered her voice.

'It'll be better,' Lindy said softly.

The small, intimate smile Hope saw the two exchange brought a lump to her throat. 'You two are staying on, then?' She felt ashamed of the envy in her heart. If anyone deserved to be happy it was Lindy.

'Sure,' Sam confirmed. 'Shall I tell her?' Hope saw his hand tighten on his wife's thigh.

'Tell me what?'

'Once I get out of the car it'll be pretty obvious,' Lindy replied drily.

Hope caught her breath. 'You're pregnant. When...?'

'Shall we just say a week later and the wedding dress wouldn't have fitted.'

'You didn't breathe a word,' Hope gasped. 'You sly pair!'

'You're supposed to say congratulations,' Sam reminded her.

'What? Oh, yes—congratulations. It's marvellous. I'm so happy for you both.' It was crazy to feel excluded, surrounded by all this happiness, but all the same... 'Am I the last to know?' She wasn't about to let the shadow of her self-pity spoil her sister's happiness. 'As usual,' she responded with mock chagrin as Lindy nodded. 'Are Mum and Dad excited?' She sat back to listen to Lindy's comical description of their parents' reactions.

Beth Lacey greeted her daughter with a passable imitation of a whirlwind.

'There's no time to waste, Hope. I've laid your clothes out—the ones you said you wanted. No, you haven't got time for a shower,' she chided as she directed her daughter firmly towards the stairs. 'Charlie, you can't possibly wear that tie!' Hope heard her mother say as she reached her bedroom.

Other than the smell of fresh paint, and the lack of

worn spots on the carpet, the house looked much the same as ever. Hand on the door handle, she let her eyes pause over-long on the spot where Alex—where she and Alex... She swallowed hard, trying to block out the steamy memories of how they'd made love just there—well, almost.

She shook her head. I've got to stop doing this she told herself firmly, he's someone else's husband now. She'd spent the last two weeks flirting wildly with every eligible male in sight. The therapy hadn't worked, but the press corps had loved the unusual photo opportunities.

Each night in her solitary room she'd cried tears that were in no way cathartic.

'You look lovely. Doesn't she, Charlie?'

'Always,' her father agreed loyally.

The tailored single-breasted suit she wore was made of olive-green wool. The Cossack-style fur fabric hat matched the trim around the collar and wrists of the jacket.

'Have Sam and Lindy already gone?'

'Don't worry, we're not late,' her mother said soothingly.

'Woman, you've never been late in your life.'

'I take it you *did* remember to get petrol?' Beth responded tartly.

Charlie Lacey raised his hand to his brow. 'Oh, God.' He grinned as the panic spread across his wife's face. 'Just teasing.'

'Why, you—!'

'If you two don't stop squabbling we *will* be late,' Hope reminded them, watching the gentle banter with a smile.

A pale wintry sun bathed the ancient stone church in soft light as they walked up the gravelled pathway.

'Hope! It's perfect now. Jake got back from his travels last night, so we're all here. Oops, watch the baby.' Anna switched her son to the opposite hip and hugged her sister. 'You're to sit with the other godparents. It's double everything with twins,' she laughed.

'Did I hear my name? Hello, beautiful.' Hope was enfolded in an enthusiastic embrace.

'Watch the hat!'

Jake was the sort of person women smiled at. The resemblance between the tall young man and Adam, his uncle, was more striking than ever.

'Like the beard,' she teased, pointing to the goatee on his chin.'

'If it makes me look sensitive and interesting, it's working.'

'Sit down, Jake,' Anna instructed imperiously. 'You make the place untidy.'

'Yes, Aunty dear,' came the meek response. 'Can Hope sit by me?' he begged as he took his seat beside his sister, Kate, and his small twin brothers.

'No, you'll bore her with your tales of adventure and danger. And it's all wildly exaggerated—he spent most of the time in youth hostels. I hope. You sit here, Hope.'

The smile at Jake's nonsense froze on her lips, but there was no humour in her startled blue eyes. Not even sisterly love or family loyalty would have brought her here if she'd suspected little Joe didn't have a substitute godfather. Alex should be on his honeymoon. What was he doing here?

She'd been standing immobile too long. It wasn't just Anna who was beginning to eye her with concern. He couldn't be here. Hallucination was one possibility that was quickly banished; he was much too substantial and *real* for that.

A baby's strident cry broke her out of her trance.

'Here, hold this one.'

Hope stiffened as the warm bundle was placed in her arms.

'Come and sit down before you drop him.'

There was only appeal in the blue eyes that fluttered to Alex's face. 'That's what I'm afraid of.'

Hope found herself squashed in beside Lindy, who wriggled closer to her husband. 'Room for one more small one,' she said to Alex.

Hope didn't know which was more distracting, the baby on her lap or the iron thigh jammed up against her. 'He's not small.'

'You're no waif yourself, angel.' The arm he'd placed across the back of the wooden pew touched her shoulders lightly. A shiver rippled through her body.

'It is cold in here, isn't it?' Lindy murmured ingeniously in a soft voice. 'Isn't he gorgeous?'

For an embarrassing instant Hope imagined that her sister was talking about Alex. She blushed hotly as she swiftly appreciated the absurdity of her error.

Light fingers lifted her hair and brushed the nape of her neck. 'You feel quite warm to me.' The faint rasp of his fingertips against her skin sent white-hot threads of longing through her trembling body. 'Young Jake seems a big fan of yours.'

'Oh, we're joined at the hip,' she snapped. 'For heaven's sake, Alex, he's a boy. I suppose you think I'm a cradle-snatcher too.' She was tired of him eagerly misinterpreting the most innocent action.

'He's a lot closer to your age than I am.' Surely there wasn't a hint of dissatisfaction in his voice. Alex? Jealous of Jake? Impossible, she told herself.

The baby in her arms made a gurgling sound and looked up at her trustfully. It was the sort of expression guaranteed to make any female all warm and mushy and Hope was no exception. I'll probably end up an old maid with cats, she thought sadly.

'Isn't he a cherub?' Lindy sighed, touching the small rounded chin of her nephew.

'Hold him if you like.'

'Can I?'

One problem solved. She wasn't a fit person to hold an infant just now. She was displaying all the classic symptoms of shock: shaking, cold sweats, a tendency to tremble and a brain that wouldn't function. Her other problem was larger and much more difficult to dispose of. She decided to wade in, regardless. 'What are you doing here?'

'I was asked to be Joe's godfather.'

'You know what I mean. Why are you wearing fluorescent green socks?' She couldn't let this detail go unmentioned any longer. The flash of colour against the sober hue of his suit was distracting.

'I told you before, I'm colour-blind. What's your excuse? Why are you so terrified of babies?'

His question distracted her from the main subject. 'What? Oh, they're so unpredictable, I suppose. And I was always so clumsy as a kid.' She frowned as she recalled her long, ungainly limbs. 'You can't drop babies. Don't change the subject.'

'You didn't drop Daphne.'

'Who's Daphne?' Lindy, who had been unashamedly eavesdropping, leaned across to ask.

Lindy didn't take the hint when Hope frowned at her. 'Orphan lamb that needed hand-rearing,' she explained in an exasperated voice.

At this point Anna returned to collect her son. 'The vicar's ready,' she told them.

The babies behaved impeccably throughout the ceremony. Hope made the required responses, all the time overpoweringly conscious of the deep baritone of the man beside her. To be thrown together on this inescapably emotional and intimate occasion was death by slow, painful inches. The battle in her beleaguered brain was titanic. He belonged to someone else, so there was no way in the world she could permit herself to respond to the searing attraction she always felt in his company. On the other hand, she didn't have any direct control over the way she felt. She wouldn't have wished this situation on her worst enemy!

'The vicar and his wife are coming back to the house with Mum and Dad. Alex says he'll take you.'

'No! No, he won't.' Let them stare. There were limits to what flesh and blood could stand. 'He'll want to be alone with his wife.' Where was Rebecca? She hadn't seen her yet amongst the press of people.

'Wife!' Anna turned to Alex with a look of shocked query, but he didn't break his thoughtful silence.

'Don't fuss, Anna. I feel like walking. It's only half a mile.'

'Walking!'

'For God's sake, you sound like a parrot.'

'You've noticed that too, have you?' Adam came up behind Hope and slipped an arm about her waist. 'Leave the girl alone, Anna, there's nothing like a brisk walk to clear jet lag.'

Jet lag might have cleared, but her other problems weren't resolved by the time she reached the Old Rectory. Try as she might to polish her tarnished scruples, she couldn't get past the number one dilemma: she loved Alex Matheson and she always would.

She stamped her shoes on the flagstones outside the door and tried to detach the stray leaf her heel had speared. The noise that spilled from the house was a warm, friendly sound. Hope had never felt so lonely in her life.

'Don't bother ringing; the French doors around this way are open.'

She stifled a cry as Alex emerged from the shadows cast by the trunk of an old gnarled tree.

'You were hiding,' she cried accusingly.

'I was waiting.' The expression in his eyes made the weakness that had begun in her legs pool in the pit of her belly. 'I was waiting for you.' She had to strain to catch the soft words.

'That was kind of you.' Impersonal was hard to achieve, but she didn't do badly—under the circumstances.

'I'm not a kind man, Hope.'

You said it, she thought bitterly. He wasn't about to make this easier. 'We'd better go in; it's cold.' She felt his presence behind her as she followed the pathway to the side of the building.

The French doors in question led to the dining room. There was a long table in the centre of the room, spread with white linen cloths and covered with a mouthwatering display of food, a fire blazed in the cast-iron grate, and a large Christmas tree was crammed with tinsel and childish trinkets.

She heard the door close softly behind her. 'I see Anna's stayed traditional,' she said, admiring the festive tree. 'This looks lovely, doesn't it? It makes you hungry just looking,' she lied brightly.

'No.'

Hope's teeth grated with exasperation. 'I'm trying...' she began. 'Oh, forget it.' Her shoulders slumped in defeat. 'You'd better be getting back to Rebecca.'

'Rebecca isn't here.'

She stared at him in astonishment. 'Where is she?'

'I don't know.'

Oh, God, had they had a falling out already? Was it her fault? 'You can't take that sort of attitude,' she told him sternly. 'I'd never have taken you for a defeatist. You've got to fight for what you want.'

'I intend to.'

The strength of conviction in this flat statement and the hard light of resolve in his eyes made her feel a lot less selfless. 'Sorry,' she said awkwardly. 'It's none of my business.'

'It's you I want,' he declared baldly. 'That kind of makes it your business.'

The hiss of her shocked inhalation sounded very loud in the room. 'How dare you say that to me?' Her voice trembled with emotion.

Alex almost carelessly trailed his finger in a bowl of avocado dip. He raised his finger to his mouth and sucked slowly and voluptuously at the creamy mixture.

It was unbearably erotic watching him. She could feel the heat creeping over her body, clouding her brain with a sensual fog. He dipped his finger in once more and offered it to her.

'Try some.' There was no mistake about it; he knew exactly what he was doing to her. Hope shook her head mutely. 'I insist. Open up, good girl,' he coaxed. His insidious voice should have carried a government health warning.

His slate-grey eyes were smoky with desire as he leaned forward in an intimate manner towards her, ignoring her small squeak of agitated protest.

'Isn't that good?' he asked throatily as he withdrew his finger. 'Did you like it?'

Like it! She took a deep, shuddering breath. 'I'll ask Mum for the recipe for you. I've got a sweet tooth myself,' she babbled.

'Then we could try—'

'Stop it Alex!' She caught hold of her hat and flung it aside. Stretching the tense muscles of her neck, she ran both hands through her hair and shook the golden cloud fiercely. 'Despite what you think, I'm not mistress material. I don't go out with married men.'

'I'm not married.'

She stopped and stared, not believing her ears. *'What?'*

'I'm not married.'

'Rebecca...'

'Rebecca married someone else, not me. In fact she married her ex-husband. She was *never* marrying me.'

'You let me think—' The anger exploded in her head. All those miserable lonely nights with only her wretched imagination as company. 'You rat!' she spat in a low, intense voice. 'You low, despicable excuse for a man!' she continued, warming to her theme. 'Have you got *any* idea what I've been going through? Of course you have,' she said, answering her own question. 'You probably enjoyed it!'

Silently he pointed to his jaw. Alex was taking her flamboyant loss of control in his stride. In fact, if she hadn't known better she would have said he looked *relieved*.

'I wouldn't lower myself,' she yelled, suspecting he was almost amused by her outburst. It was tempting, though—so tempting.

Her hands balled into fists at her sides. Inspiration came in a flash. She reached forward and grabbed a fistful of the pale green dip and flung it at him. All her pent-up emotions went into the gesture. With an open mouth she watched it drip down the front of his charcoal-grey jacket onto his polished leather shoes.

He looked down expressionlessly. 'Feel better?' He flicked the buttons of his jacket open with an expression of distaste.

'I was aiming for your face.'

'What you need is a steady hand.'

Hope let out a shriek of protest as the cream hit her nose dead centre. 'Why, you...!'

'Oh, no, you don't.' The hand she'd refilled with viscous mess was captured in an iron grip. She found herself firmly propelled backwards until she was pinned against the wall. She aimed a few wild kicks, several of which collided with his shins, before she finally subsided, her chest heaving with emotion.

'If this is going to be a contact sport,' she complained, panting hard, 'I think you've got an unfair weight advantage. Let me go, Alex,' she said, eyeing the closed door nervously. If anyone walked in now... 'I'm a mess. I've got to get cleaned up.' Now that her temper had begun to subside she could appreciate how embarrassing her present position was.

'Let me.' He pulled a handkerchief from his pocket and began to wipe the sticky mess from her face. Even though her hands were free, Hope didn't move as he tenderly dabbed her face clean. 'It's in your hair. Such lovely hair.' His light touch and soft words spun a gossamer web of sensual lethargy.

'It's not natural, you know. I have highlights in the winter.' His expression scared her. Or was it her own eager response to the primal hunger in his eyes that scared her more? 'And I dye my eyelashes.'

'Now she tells me.'

'This isn't a joke, Alex.'

'It's disillusioning,' he admitted, 'but...'

'This isn't funny,' she protested weakly as his fingers moved down the graceful curve of her throat. 'I hate you.'

Alex's questing fingers discovered a sticky area on her throat. 'I missed a bit.' Then he applied his tongue to the area in question. It was only his hands under her armpits that stopped her sliding to the floor. The sensations that ripped through her body were scalding.

'The best syllabub I've ever tasted.' Hope willed her knees to take her weight as Alex placed his hands flat against the wall on either side of her head. 'Do you want to try some?'

His throaty offer planted a clear image in Hope's mind of her lapping up the sticky confection before it melted on the warm surface of his skin. 'No!' she gasped, as though he'd just made an indecent suggestion.

'I thought you were more adventurous than that.' The mocking note in his low, frankly wicked chuckle would have made her protest strongly had he not fused their lower bodies together without warning.

'You're a very bad man,' she said huskily. The pressure against the sensitive area of her groin was indescribable. It offered her a small degree of comfort to know that his desire was no less urgently agonising.

'I will be bad if that's what you like,' he promised throatily.

'It's you I like,' she cried suddenly. 'Oh, Alex.' With a sob she linked her fingers behind his head and kissed him. A growl reverberated low in his throat as his lips parted to admit the determined trespass of her tongue.

Hope twisted sinuously to press her body closer to his. 'You can keep the syllabub—I'll eat you.' The arms around her ribcage tightened painfully as she whispered brokenly in his ear.

'Uncle Adam said we couldn't start eating until everyone was ready. Why are they allowed to?'

'Just look, Uncle Sam. They've made a mess too,' an identical voice added.

Hope stared helplessly back at the accusing stares of Adam's identical twin nephews, one of whom sat on the shoulders of Sam Rourke.

'We... We...' She cast a wild look of appeal towards Alex.

'We were hungry.' Alex met her reproachful glare with a very definite sink-or-swim expression.

'So much for chivalry! Thanks a lot. And if you laugh again, Sam Rourke, I'll...' She planted her hands on her hips and glared at him resentfully.

'Sam, you'll have to keep these two away from the food or there won't be—' Anna stopped, her eyes widening as she took in the implications of the scene before her. 'Oh, this is where you got to, Hope. I was about to send Adam out to find you.'

'Alex found her. And the poor girl was starving, so he—'

'Sam!' Anna said, trying unsuccessfully to restrain her laughter.

'I'm so glad I was able to provide you all with entertainment,' Hope choked. 'Don't let it worry you that it's at my expense. I thought *you* at least had more tact,' she said to Sam.

This was too much for Anna, who folded up as laughter shook her.

'I'm going to clean up,' Hope said with icy dignity.

'I'd take the back stairs if I were you,' her sister called after her.

Hope followed this advice.

She stared at her reflection in the mirror and tried to sort out her jumbled thoughts. He wasn't married. That wasn't the only change in circumstances. He wasn't under any illusions about how she felt either. It was a bit late to cultivate an air of mystery after she'd virtually ravished the man.

'What happens next?' she asked out loud. She spun around as she saw the flicker of movement on the periphery of her vision. 'You! How did you get in?' She'd definitely locked the door.

Alex waved a key at her. 'Anna gave it to me. This bathroom is shared by two rooms, remember.

'My sister's nothing but a rotten traitor.'

'If she hadn't provided the key I'd have battered down the door.' This wasn't macho posturing; he was simply stating a fact. 'If I'd followed you the last time you ran off we'd both have been saved two weeks of hell.'

Hell? He'd been in hell? This news made her feel suddenly optimistic. 'Colorado at this time of the year is delightful. I even got a chance to ski.'

'I know. I saw the pictures in the gossip columns. Is it the financier or the European prince you're going to marry? There was some dispute over that.'

'Neither!'

'I think you're probably wise,' he agreed smoothly. 'He was a very minor prince, and the rich guy's dollars couldn't buy him a chin.'

If she hadn't felt so tongue-tied she'd have done something to deflate his intolerable confidence. 'What do you think you're doing?'

'Locking the door. So we won't be disturbed.' He proceeded to block the door which still *did* have a key with his broad-shouldered bulk.

'Give me that key—immediately!'

'If you want it—get it.' She stared incredulously as he dropped it deliberately down the front of his conservative grey trousers.

'*Alex!*' she said in strangled voice. 'I can't believe you just did that.'

'I know it's not original. Women in those old forties movies dropped vital items down their cleavages all the time. Call this my bid for equality between the sexes. Blushes like that can't do your sophisticated image any good.'

'You're the only one who makes me blush.'

'That's nice,' he said with a smug smile.

'It's not at all nice,' she contradicted hotly. 'It's awful. You specialise in putting me at a disadvantage.'

'It feels like that because you love me.'

'I *what?*' she squeaked in a strangled voice. She worked really hard to achieve a scornful expression, but her facial muscles wouldn't co-operate. He knows! God, of course he knows, she told herself angrily. I haven't been exactly subtle.

'You heard me. And I'm not opening this door until you admit it.'

'You're the most arrogant man I've ever met.'

'You'll get used to it. I'm too old to change.'

He wasn't going to start on that tired old age-gap theme, was he? 'You're not too old for anything—' She stopped, an arrested expression stealing over her face. 'What do you mean, I'll get used to it?' she asked cautiously.

'We don't have to get married straight away. Or not at all, if you prefer it that way.' Why hadn't she seen it before? Under the casual nonchalance he was as uncertain as she was, and feeling his way just as tentatively. This revelation put quite a different slant on his behaviour.

'Is this a proposal?'

'I can't ask you to marry me, Hope.'

After all this? Don't let him be married after all, she prayed. 'Why not?'

'I can't take the risk of you saying no. I'm not sure how I'd live my life if you weren't part of it—the most important part.'

Nobody had *ever* looked at her that way. She felt as if she'd explode with sheer happiness and relief.

'Say *something,*' he growled.

She couldn't respond. Her throat was closed over with emotion and her mind was still stunned with the power of his blunt declaration.

'You think this is *funny?*' You laid your heart and soul on the line for a woman and she laughed. 'I'll—'

'Strangling me would defeat the objective, wouldn't it? Oh, Alex, I'm not laughing—I'm crying,' she sniffed, blotting her shining eyes with the back of her hand. 'With happiness, you idiot,' she cried lovingly.

'Thank God for that,' he breathed. His shoulders slumped with relief and he held out his arms.

With a sob, Hope walked straight into them. They closed around her as though he'd never let her go. A scenario Hope could find no immediate fault with.

'Oh, Alex, I love you.' Her heart-felt declaration chased away the last shadow of vulnerability from his face.

'I told you so.' There was a fierce, predatory gleam of satisfaction in his eyes as he kissed her hungrily.

'Hold on, hold on,' he said, drawing away slightly. 'Let's get something straight. You're not just after me for my body?' His laughing eyes were narrowed suspiciously

'Are you playing hard to get?' It was strange to get used to a man who could lift her off the ground and swing her around as though she was a featherweight.

'A man's got his pride.'

'I haven't,' she said huskily, the smile fading from her lips. 'Not where you're concerned. I've spent the last week thinking you were married to Rebecca. How could you let me think…?'

'Honestly, love, when I bribed Jonathan to bring you to the restaurant that night, I didn't think for a second you'd jump to that conclusion.'

'You *bribed* Jon?'

Alex winced. 'That sort of slipped out. If you must know, I had to see you—and that was the best way I could think of doing it.'

'What did you bribe Jon with?'

'There's a waiting list of nearly five years for the Matheson model he wants and Harkness was on the bottom of it. He's driving round in a shiny new sports car today.'

'That's corrupt!'

'Let's not be hasty. That's expedient. To get you I was prepared to bend the rules a lot further than that.'

She wouldn't have been human if she hadn't been flattered by the elaborate lengths he'd been prepared to go to see her. She accepted the ruthless streak in his personality, knowing it was always tempered by a sensitive, generous aspect.

'You let me carry on thinking...' His taut, mobile mouth fascinated her.

'You got drunk—remember? I had a hard enough time just protecting you from my less chivalrous instincts without trying to explain things when your mental processes were a bit...challenged. I don't know how I kept my hands off you that night,' he confessed huskily. 'In the morning I was about to tell you when you decided to throw up.' The memory still had the power to bring raw frustration to his voice. 'It wasn't very encouraging.'

'I expect that put you off.'

'I was too desperate by that point to be worried about timing. You have no idea what sort of hellish night I'd just spent. I fully intended following you when you locked yourself in your room, but Miranda advised me to give you time to cool down. Great advice that turned out to be—the next day she wouldn't even tell me where you'd gone.'

'I made her promise,' Hope said guiltily.

'I only found out when your *après-ski* antics hit the gossip columns.'

'Oh, that.' She gave a small grimace. 'I was trying to forget you.'

'Successfully?'

'Don't look so smug. I'm moderately surprised you didn't assume I was sleeping with the entire Winter Olympics squad.'

'They were there too, were they? You *did* have a good time.'

'Some of them. And I had a miserable time, as you well know. You know what I mean, Alex—after the way you reacted over Lloyd.'

'What did you expect, Hope? I was a man who'd fallen in love.' She pounced on the confession and hugged it to her. He loves me—Alex really loves me!

'I've never been very good at concessions, not with standards, either in my personal or professional life. And what happens? I meet you and I redefine my criteria on an almost daily basis to justify continuing our relationship. I was in a downward spiral and blaming you every step of the way. I was beginning to wonder just how far I'd go to continue sleeping with you when I found out you'd been lying to me all along. It was the final straw. I felt betrayed. It was never *you* I couldn't forgive; it was my own weakness. I convinced myself it was all a game to you, that you'd been laughing at me all along.'

'I wished so many times I'd never started the charade, but I'd promised Lloyd I'd keep quiet.' She laid a hand on his shoulder and felt the tension in his rigid muscles. 'I suppose I just wanted you to trust me.'

'I was half out of my mind with jealousy, Hope. No matter what I told myself, I couldn't stop wanting you.'

Hope gave a rueful smile and ruffled his thick hair tenderly. 'I know what that feels like. Rebecca was *nice*, which made it worse. I wanted to hate her and I couldn't even do that.' Her nails pressed into the soft flesh of her palms as she recalled the agony she'd felt.

'I've known Rebecca for years, and Alain, her husband. I was best man at their wedding—the first time around. About eighteen months ago he walked out on her for a younger woman. She was devastated, and everyone who knew them was shocked rigid. They were the perfect couple fairy tales are made of. The break wasn't a clean one. Alain didn't just keep in touch, he was constantly on the doorstep. It was as if he didn't want to let go. Rebecca reached breaking point, and I told Alain straight that he wasn't being fair to her. How the hell was she supposed to start a new life if he was there, constantly reminding her of what she'd lost?'

'I bet that went down well.'

'Anyone who tells you you don't have to take sides in a divorce is a liar,' Alex responded drily.

'They got back together?'

Alex nodded. 'I hope it works out, but it won't be easy for either of them. Love may not conquer all, but it sure as hell helps.'

'I love you, Alex.' She felt delirious with pleasure at her freedom to make the admission, to make it twenty times a day if she wanted to. 'I hope you won't get bored hearing me say that.'

He caught his breath at the expression that glowed in her eyes. 'I just hope I can live up to your expectations. I'm not an easy man, Hope. And I did say some vicious things to you. It's no excuse, but it was a tremendous shock suddenly not being emotionally in control of my life,' he continued in a driven voice. 'I felt as if you were playing the tune and I was dancing. I fought against it. In my ignorance, I imagined things would go back to normal,' he recalled with a short, hard laugh. 'If I'm honest, I think a perverse part of me leapt at the chance to take control, even if that meant driving you away. I was a fool and a coward, Hope.' His eyes blazed with emotion as he gazed at her. 'I couldn't have been more wrong.'

'I'm pretty used to making my own decisions and getting my own way too, Alex. Letting someone close is new for me too.' She didn't want him to paint her as the victim in all this. Misunderstandings had been on both sides.

'Don't get me wrong, I never resented your strength. Strong women don't threaten me—I'm attracted by independence. It was the changes in *me* I couldn't adapt to. I've always been self-sufficient. External factors have never had the power, except in the most superficial way, to influence my...' He shrugged. 'For want of a better word, my happiness. I guess, in my arrogance, I thought I was the exception to the rule—the one man who *was* an island. Then you came along.' He placed his hands on her shoulders and looked deeply into her eyes.

'I'll never abuse that, Alex.' She was deeply moved that he wasn't holding anything back, and she didn't underestimate how much it had cost him to lower his defences so totally.

'I took a long, hard look at myself and I didn't like what I saw. How could I have believed all those things about you when at every turn I could see your warmth and openness?' He groaned, self-recrimination clear on his face. 'If only I'd accepted my first gut instinct instead of trying to find a flaw. Lloyd was right—you are pure gold.'

She made a sound of protest. 'Don't, Alex.' She couldn't bear to see him hurting. 'I like what I see when I look at you. I did the instant I saw you at Lindy's wedding.' Later she'd show him the photos of that day, the ones she'd kept back for herself. Well-thumbed prints that so recently had been all she'd thought she'd ever have of him. But now...! Now her heart felt as if it would explode with joy.

'I know.' The old steel that she loved was back in his eyes. He took hold of her left hand, his eyes admiring the elegant length of her tapering fingers. 'I think I first realised what had happened to me when you begged me not to leave you after the accident. I'd have given anything to take away your hurt. I've never felt so helpless in my life.' His voice throbbed with emotion and his eyes darkened. 'And I was responsible.'

'That's not true,' she contradicted firmly. 'What happened to you, Alex?' She needed to hear him say it. It would all seem more real then.

He ran a hand through his hair. 'You mean I haven't told you?' A wry grin twisted his lips. 'Hope Lacey, I love you and always will. Shall we get married or live in sin, my love?'

'Sin with you sounds attractive,' she said, lacing her fingers with his. 'Only I think I'm a conventional girl at heart. Do you mind?'

'Mind!' His smouldering eyes ran over her face. 'I want all the world to know you're mine.'

'Perhaps we should just limit ourselves to the family today,' she suggested with a cheeky grin. 'Heavens!' Her eyes opened wide in consternation. 'They'll all be wondering what we're doing.'

Alex didn't seem in any hurry to release her. 'You've forgotten something.'

'I have?'

'The key,' he said with a lecherous grin.

She wasn't about to spoil his fun or hers by pointing out that one door at least still had a perfectly good key in the lock. 'That is a problem,' she agreed innocently.

'I think it's one we should investigate as a matter of urgency.'

'My thoughts exactly.' She enjoyed the instant effect her sultry smile had on him.

'Aunty Hope, have you got locked in?'

'We did that once and Jake got us out. Shall we get Jake for you?'

Hope paused, her lips a mere whisper from Alex's mouth. 'I don't believe this.'

'If you don't say something they're going to drag Jake up here.'

This reminder spurred Hope into action. 'No, boys, I'll be right out. Don't get Jake. You can go back downstairs.'

'No, we want to use the bathroom.'

'Why this bathroom?' she breathed, rolling her eyes skyward.

'I think we'd better admit defeat. It's amazing people actually *want* these little monsters, isn't it?'

'Children? Don't you? I mean—' She broke off, flushing. It would be ironic if just when her maternal instincts had kicked in—a little late—it turned out Alex didn't want children.

'The truth is,' he admitted cautiously, 'I'm as crazy about them as the next man. Don't worry, though, if you don't like the idea. Your career...'

'Oh, but I do—now.' She hastily filled his awkward pause. He'd actually be willing to forgo children for her? The depth of his love made her feel humble. 'I'm not really the earth mother type,' she warned him. 'You won't come home to the smell of fresh bread baking and rows of rosy-cheeked children.' She didn't want to raise false expectations. 'To tell you the truth, I'm not that great with tiny babies—but children I'm fine with. I'd quite like to have a bash—at least once—if you're game?'

'I think you're beautiful with babies. Don't worry, love, the rate your sisters are going you'll get a lot of practice before your time comes.'

'That's true. Mind you, at this rate there's not much risk of me getting pregnant,' she observed with frustration.

'I always pay my debts. I promised you a customised orgy with individual instruction, and come hell or high water—'

'We've already done those,' she reminded him with a grin.

'I'll deliver the goods.'

Hope smiled lovingly up at him, her colour heightened. 'I'm relying on it.'

Set in the steamy Australian outback
a fabulous new triology by
bestselling Presents author

Emma Darcy

Kings of the
Outback

Three masterful brothers
and the women who tame them

On sale June 2000
THE CATTLE KING'S MISTRESS
Harlequin Presents®, #2110

On sale July 2000
THE PLAYBOY KING'S WIFE
Harlequin Presents®, #2116

On sale August 2000
THE PLEASURE KING'S BRIDE
Harlequin Presents®, #2122

Available wherever Harlequin books are sold.

HARLEQUIN®
Makes any time special ™

Visit us at www.eHarlequin.com HPKING